Big Pharma, Big Drama

Managing is not a game

Laurence Sellin

Big Pharma, Big Drama

Managing is not a game

Yanaël Marceau's investigations
Volume 2

Detective novel

Éditions Polar Impulse

By the same author
published at Éditions Polar Impulse

L'affaire de la Rue Soufflot - Entre meprise et emprise, January 2023, 155 pp.

A Case For The Paris Police - Between Misunderstanding And Control, Detective Novel, British English Version, May 2023, 155 pp.

A Case For The Paris Police - Between Misunderstanding And Control, Thriller, American English Version, May 2023, 155 pp.

Discover the author

You can discover my literary world and my characters on my self-published author's website

https://www.editionspolarimpulse.com/

in particular at this web address

https://www.editionspolarimpulse.com/auteur_personnages.html/

If you wish to contact me, please send an e-mail to

contact@editionspolarimpulse.com

Legal information

ISBN: 978-2-487394-00-1
Paperback version published by Éditions Polar Impulse for Laurence Sellin
Sold at the single price of AUS$16,50/£8.99/9,99 €/
1st edition - Legal Deposit – December 2023

Cover design, illustration, and photo: Nathalie GLÉVAREC
https://www.graphistelitteraire.fr

Logo credits : GraphicSprings
https://www.graphicsprings.com/

Interior layout support: Book Design Template
https://www.bookdesigntemplates.com/

Printing: Amazon KDP print-on-demand service
Printed in Australia/Europe/United Kingdom by Amazon KDP— December 2023

*Living means above all keeping your cool
and forcing yourself to bounce back from the unpredictable.*

Douglas KENNEDY.

Extract from the author's preface

Compilation *Mes Héroïnes*

Éditions Omnibus, 2015, p. VII.

Table of Contents

Arnaud Wagram,
a tormented psychiatrist

December 2023 – Toulouse (France).

MY NAME IS ARNAUD WAGRAM. I am fifty years old. I have been a freelance psychiatrist in Toulouse for twenty years, specialising in psychotraumatology.

After studying medicine at the Toulouse III-Paul Sabatier Faculty of Science, I took up this profession at the age of thirty out of a sense of vocation.

Today, overwhelmed by remorse and guilt, I have decided to unscrew my plaque and put an end to this practice for good.

Faced with these negative feelings, which have been assailing me day and night for the last three months, I know I should seek help, but when you have been used to looking after others, it's not easy to admit your own suffering and confide it to someone else, even less to a fellow member.

How did I end up in this untenable situation, having built a loving, close-knit family and, as an adult, having worked in the occupation I had chosen when I was a teenager?

That is the story I'm going to tell you now, in the hope that the words I put down on paper will have a therapeutic effect that will help me to escape it.

Chapter One

Two and a half years of therapy

December 2023,
Arnaud Wagram's recounting
of events that took place
from April 2018 to September 2020.

I N APRIL 2018, I had a new patient in my practice, Lauriane Emans, aged twenty-four. My secretary had noted her name in my diary, this morning, and when I checked my appointments for the day, her name vaguely reminded me of something, but I couldn't remember exactly who she was.

At the start of the session, she explained why she felt the need for psychiatric treatment, and shared with me a letter written by a colleague at the Cochin Hospital, whom she had consulted during her last weeks in Paris, in February and March 2018, before moving to Toulouse.

These various pieces of information told me that Lauriane Emans had been the unfortunate victim of the Soufflot Street case which had hit the headlines, and even triggered a media frenzy, at the start of the new academic year in September 2017.

As I listened to her talk about the case and the stigmas it had caused her, I tried to recall what I had heard at the time: the victim had just completed a master's degree in law at *La Sorbonne*, bringing to an end five years of brilliant higher education, partly at the Toulouse law school and partly in Paris, where she had moved in September 2015. After her bachelor's degree, she had decided to specialise for two years on a master's course, and thanks to a satisfactory academic record, she had been able to gain admission to one of the most prestigious law faculties in Paris. Her last two years at university had gone smoothly, without any special event to spoil her success.

Lauriane Emans went on to explain to me that it was on her return home from her graduation ceremony that she had been attacked: the owner of the building had dealt her several violent blows, one of which, to the head, had caused her concussion and left her in a coma for five months, from September 2017 to February 2018.

When she had woken up, she had been visited by a lieutenant from the Third Judicial Police Department and the criminal psychologist assisting the investigators, both of whom had come to take her testimony as one of the main acts in an investigation that was still underway. On this occasion, they had explained to her the motive behind what had to be called an attempted murder: the owner of the building had wanted to comply with the wishes of one of his tenants, who, having taken a sudden dislike to Lauriane Emans since she had moved in two years earlier, had developed a delusion of persecution towards her. The person who had carried out these dreadful acts, finding himself under the control of this tenant, had added to the horror and the young woman, who was not yet my patient at the time, had found herself, alone in her home, in a life-threatening emergency.

The two investigators had then explained to her that she had been saved *in extremis* thanks to the intervention of one of her ambulance drivers, who had come to pick her up from her home at Soufflot Street to take her to a physiotherapy session. When his calls had remained unanswered, he had alerted the first aid rescuers who, after entering her flat through the window, had discovered the crime scene and had activated the usual rescue procedures in such a situation.

Lauriane Emans also explained to me that, when she had been questioned on her hospital bed in February 2018, the investigators had informed her of the worrying disappearance of this ambulance driver a few days after he had saved her life. Two months after learning of this tragic news, she thought that this aspect of the case continued to be at a standstill, although she told me that, before leaving Paris, she had tried to find out more about it from the missing man's colleagues. They hadn't been able to give her any information, apart from the fact that they themselves had been heard by investigators from the Third Judicial Police Department within a very short space of time after this disappearance.

During our first consultation, Lauriane Emans told me that she was very worried about this ambulance driver, with whom she had built bonds of friendship and trust, over the twelve months prior to her attack, as he had taken her to her physiotherapy sessions on several occasions. Not knowing what had become of him after this short news item and the media hype it had given rise to, and having received no news of him since her recovery from the coma, she imagined the worst: she thought that, because he had come to her aid, his partner might, out of jealousy, have wanted to take his life. So she confided in me that she felt responsible for any misfortune that might have happened to her friend at the time.

As I couldn't remember the details of the case, I asked her why she already had to have physiotherapy sessions before she had been attacked, noting that she had come to my office in an electric wheelchair. She explained that a lack of oxygen at birth had caused her brain damage, which in turn had resulted in a loss of motor function in her lower limbs. When I asked her how she operated on a day-to-day basis in these conditions, she explained that, with the exception of some food shopping that she bought once a week from local shops, she carried out a large number of tasks remotely, such as buying large quantities of groceries from a home delivery company, practising her professional activity of transcribing meetings, and buying digital books and series on DVD, which meant that she rarely went out.

With my twenty years' experience in mental pathology, I wondered whether this specific behaviour was due to her lack of mobility, or whether the fact that she didn't go out could hide a deeper psychological disorder. According to the latter hypothesis, she would have behaved in the same way had she not been a person with reduced mobility. However, as it was still too early to ask her, I decided to keep this information in the back of my mind until I could see how she would develop during her therapy.

At the end of this hour's contact, we scheduled another consultation for the following week, and, in the meantime, I looked up information on the Internet about the Soufflot Street case. A number of neighbours living in the building where this news item had taken place had reported that this tenant was not very sociable: during the two years she had lived there, no one had really known what she did for a living, whether she received friends, and so on. The only thing they knew for sure was that she moved using a wheelchair and that her next-door neighbour had taken a sudden dislike to her. The residents interviewed at the time had been unable to explain the process that had led to this tragedy. At the same time, they had explained having been shocked by the tragic outcome of this more or less latent conflict, in which no one had wanted to get involved.

In my opinion, no one orders the attempted murder of a vulnerable person for no reason, but as I wasn't able to access to the investigation file containing the criminal psychologist's report on the case, I decided to look into the matter with Lauriane Emans when I saw her the following week. She explained that she had spent her childhood with her maternal grandparents, in a single-parent family, and that she had spent her teenage years with her mother and her mother's husband, who had acknowledged her when she was nine, even though he was not her father. These particular circumstances would have meant a change of name, a change of school and a change of environment that she would have coped with more or less successfully, even if the latter was only a few kilometres from her grandparents' house where she had always lived. I understood that so many changes at once, in the life of a nine-year-old child, hadn't been easy to integrate, but I also thought that they couldn't have been enough to justify a personality disorder that could lead the subject to become the victim of an assassination attempt, fourteen years later, as she entered adulthood.

As I mentioned this to her, she recalled the hardness of her mother's husband's character, incompatible with her particular sensitivity as an intellectually precocious child, which no one in her close circle had taken into account. According to her interpretation, this uncomfortable situation had led her to withdraw progressively into her inner world, failing to find any other solution. Having only younger half-brothers with whom there was a big age difference, and no uncle or aunt with whom she could have felt emotionally close and to whom she could have confided her distress, she told me that, at the end of her childhood and throughout her adolescence, she had taken refuge in her books, building an imaginary world when the real world had been too difficult for her to bear. Because of her physical disability, and the fact that she couldn't play any sport, she hadn't been able to find a confidant in a peer group either, even though this kind of contact is usually much sought after at this stage of life.

To gauge the extent of her emotional loneliness, I asked her if she had any friends. She told me that, during her years at university, she had tried to meet one new friend a year, but in the end she had only one left, and she came back to her ambulance driver friend, whom she thought had disappeared because of her, and whom she seemed to miss very much. Given her mental state and her physical handicap, modesty prevented me from asking her if she had a boyfriend, or if she was thinking of setting up home, in the next few years, but my rather realistic position as a doctor led me to expect a negative answer to this question.

At the end of this second interview, faced with what seemed to me to be a post-traumatic depression due to her attack and to the unexplained disappearance of her ambulance driver friend, I decided to see her once a fortnight, in consultation. This therapy was to last two and a half years, from April 2018 to September 2020. During this period, the trial of the Soufflot Street case also took place. On this occasion, I learnt a piece of information that was crucial to the events I am about to relate, and which I had suspected before receiving official confirmation: at the time of her attack, Lauriane Emans was suffering from schizoid personality disorder, from which she is still suffering today, six years later. In concrete terms, schizoid personality disorder means inability, more or less marked depending on the situation, to make social contact with other people, the sufferer preferring to take refuge in his or her inner world rather than make any effort to socialise.

During these two and a half years of therapy, I did everything in my power as a mental health practitioner to make her aware of her disorder. My aim was then to try and gradually reduce these effects on her personality, so as to enable her to better manage her social contacts which, even if she didn't seek them out, are inevitable in any civilised society. However, like all sufferers of this personality disorder, Lauriane Emans, feeling particularly at ease in her inner world, wasn't able to understand where the problem was located: she continued, more or less consciously, to make a complete mockery of what others might think of her and of the way she operated, often going against normal practice. I sometimes wondered whether the nonconformity she displayed was not overplayed.

So, when I asked her several times whether she was thinking of going on holiday during the summer months to enjoy the fresh air of the sea or of the ocean, she always replied in the negative, saying that she preferred writing detective novels in her spare time rather than wasting it doing things for which she saw no point. I suggested that she should write detective novels and enjoy her holidays away from home, as I didn't think the two activities were incompatible. She replied that the periods of voluntary lockdown to her home during her holidays gave her an inspiration that she didn't think she would be able to find elsewhere, while allowing her to take her mind off her routine job of transcribing meetings. Not having her talent or inspiration to write novels myself, I confess I couldn't find a rational answer to this unstoppable argument.

To help her escape from emotional loneliness, I advised her to sign up for group activities in which she might have found an interest, such as taking part in a face-to-face writing workshop, for example. Lauriane Emans never followed this advice, explaining to me that many such workshops existed online and that, because of her passion for writing novels, she had already attended them all with the aim of becoming as high-return as possible at this activity.

Finally, to help her socialise, I also advised her to stop working from home and to join a company where she could transcribe meetings, which she would have attended in the same way as the others, even if she didn't speak at those occasions. To this end, in June 2020, I proposed to her that I forward her CV to a friend of mine from the university, a doctor of pharmacy and director of the French subsidiary of a private American laboratory specialising in research and development in the field of innovative health technologies. As the subsidiary's head office was in Paris, Lauriane had to accept the idea of having to return to the capital to live, which wasn't easy given the tragedy she had experienced there during the Soufflot Street case. Together, after months of therapy, we managed to get her over this hurdle.

Then she also had to come to terms with the idea of working as part of a group, with all the concessions that implies in terms of social contacts. In order to make it easier for her to accept these concessions, I tried to get her to see the material advantages she could gain from being recruited on contract in a large company, whereas her status as a freelance transcriber only provided her with a fluctuating income in proportion to the work she did each month. But she didn't seem very receptive to this argument, replying that the material aspects of life were of little interest to her, as long as she could devote herself to her three passions: reading, writing and watching crime series on DVD.

Finally, after a great deal of discussion, arguments and counter-arguments, Lauriane Emans accepted the idea of working for this company, which recruited her on an open-ended contract on Tuesday, 1st September 2020.

At the time, I was delighted that she had finally agreed to follow my advice, whose the purpose was to help her overcome her post-traumatic depression and improve her psychological health by implementing resocialisation techniques. Nevertheless, given the tragic events that unfolded over the next three years, today, in December 2023, I am terribly angry with myself for having given her this advice and for having acted as an intermediary in her recruitment. These terrible events have been making me feel inwardly sick ever since I first heard about them.

Indeed, I have been worrying myself sick to such an extent that I have decided to put an end to my work as a freelance psychiatrist for good.

I am now going to tell you this story.

Chapter 2

A crime in Paris

O N MONDAY, 4TH SEPTEMBER 2023, Lauriane Emans came back to my office for a consultation, at her request.

With the exception of best wishes for the New Year emails that we exchanged, at her initiative, in January of each of the last three years, we had had no other contact since she had been recruited by the laboratory in September 2020, at the end of her therapy.

So I was surprised to see her again, not as a tourist on holiday, but as a patient. That day, she seemed even more physically scarred by something that was tormenting her than the first time I had seen her in my office, in April 2018, after the Soufflot Street case.

I asked her what the reason was for her visit and she explained that, during her permanent contract with the laboratory, she had become the source for an investigative journalist, who was an independent press correspondent in Paris for various American newspapers, which had put her in an unbearable situation. Remembering her tendency to retreat into her inner world, due to the schizoid personality disorder she suffered from and which my first therapy had failed to cure, I imagined that, during this recent period of her life in Paris, she had only had to leave her flat to go to work, do a few weekly food shopping trips and to go to her physiotherapy sessions – in other words, the minimum number of outings required because you have to work, eat and look after yourself in order to live. So I asked her what she had found so interesting to tell an American press correspondent in Paris.

In answer to my question, she told me that he had been shot in the head in cold blood on 3rd May 2022, as he was leaving his home in the fourteenth district to go to the scene of a news report.

In response to this convoluted answer, I asked her if she was still writing detective novels and if she wasn't developing a split personality between the characters she invented in her novels and the people she came into contact with in real life.

Getting upset by the fact that I didn't believe her, she replied that schizoid personality disorder had nothing to do with mythomania or invention. She also told me that all I had to do was to check the veracity of her words on the Internet by typing the name of the journalist in question, Benjamin Marshall, into a search engine, which I did immediately. I then came across an article summarising the commencement of the investigation, written by a journalist specialising in short news items for a major French national daily newspaper.

This article, dated Saturday, 7th May 2022, reported the following facts:

AMERICAN JOURNALIST MURDERED IN THE HEART OF PARIS: AN UPDATE ON THE INVESTIGATION SO FAR

"On Tuesday, 3rd May, 2022, at 8 a.m., as he left his home located in Rue Daguerre, in the fourteenth district of Paris, to go to the scene of a news report, Benjamin Marshall, a freelance press correspondent

for various American newspapers, in Paris, was shot in the head in cold blood.

The emergency services were alerted by residents who had witnessed the violence of the events as they left their homes at the start of the day. They came across the tragedy just minutes after it had occurred, only to find that the victim had died.

The Paris Public Prosecutor and the investigators from the Third Judicial Police Department, who were responsible for the area, were called forthwith to the scene of the crime by the Judicial Police Regional Management Headquarters. Every effort must be made to avoid a diplomatic crisis between France and the United States following the brutal death of an American citizen on French territory. Furthermore, as the President of the Republic and his wife, accompanied with by a delegation of French business leaders, are due to make an official visit to the United States from 30th of November to 2nd of December, the Minister of the Interior has already pointed out to Superintendent Langlois, Head of the Third Judicial Police Department, that it would be highly desirable for this investigation to be resolved before this State visit takes place.

It was against this background of extreme political tension that the first investigations were carried out. Firstly, the Criminal Records Office was immediately called to the scene of the crime and took photos of the surrounding area and of the body before it was transported, still warm, to the Paris mortuary, where a post-mortem was carried out later that day. Criminal investigation technicians also took samples in and around the crime scene on Rue Daguerre, in order to find clues leading back to the killer. During the autopsy, the forensic pathologist photographed the wound and drew a diagram of it. In his report, the latter pointed out that, according to the angle at which the bullet penetrated the victim's body, the shot had been fired by a sniper from high ground and using a long-range weapon.

Following the autopsy, the ballistics experts attempted to establish the characteristics of the bullet taken from the victim's body, but as it had no particular striation marks, they were unable to search the files to determine which weapon it might have come from.

It is on the basis of these very slim technical elements that the officers of the Third Judicial Police Department are carrying out the investigation: as they have no clues leading to trace the killer, they have decided to focus their investigations on the victim and his background."

After reading this article, I told Lauriane Emans that I still didn't see the link between her work for the laboratory and the offending facts. However, she continued in the same vein as before, recounting to me that she felt responsible for the murder of this investigative journalist, which she claimed had occurred as a result of the revelations she had confided in him during the Christmas holidays of 2021–2022 about the laboratory she was working for at the time.

As I myself was originally responsible for her recruitment in this company, whose director is a friend of mine, I wondered what staggering revelations she could have confided to this journalist to the point that he was murdered. I also wondered whether the stress caused by this recruitment had not caused her a paranoid psychosis consisting of perceived enemies, or dangers, where none existed.

Finally, I noticed that when people around her suddenly or unexpectedly disappeared or died, she tended to blame herself. In my time with her as a patient, this was the second time she believed herself to be responsible for the tragic disappearance of someone she knew.

I asked her to explain to me the sequence of events that had led to her becoming a source for this journalist. She told me that to do so, she had to go back to May 2022, when the criminal investigation into the case began, in order to tell me exactly what she had told the investigators from the Third Judicial Police Department responsible for the case.

Chapter 3

Benjamin Marshall, the victim

May 2022,

Bastion Street - Third Judicial Police Department

Paris 17th District.

Daguerre Street- Victim's home,

Paris 14th District.

THE CRIME SCENE INVESTIGATION did not yield any usable information for the investigators from the Third Judicial Police Department. So they decided to concentrate on the victim, Benjamin Marshall, and his environment.

The investigation team consisted of Police Commander Cédric Zandowski, a rank to which he had been promoted in 2019, after twelve years of service, at the age of thirty-seven. Since the early retirement of Commander Lionel Fresnay in 2021, after having completed twenty-five years' service, he had become group leader of this investigation unit. His team was composed of Yanaël Marceau, the young criminal investigation Lieutenant made famous in 2017 by the solving of the Soufflot Street case. In 2021, at the age of twenty-nine, after four years of service, he had attained the rank of police inspector and had also become the group's procedural expert.

The Commander and the Inspector worked under the supervision of Superintendent Étienne Langlois, who had been managing the Third Judicial Police Department for ten years. A new lieutenant was due to be recruited to the team, but the Superintendent seemed in no hurry to fulfil this obligation, preferring to delegate it to his successor. After having completed thirty-five years' service, at the age of sixty, he was only looking forward to a well-deserved retirement, which he was due to take on 31st December 2022. So when the Third Judicial Police Department had been asked to investigate the murder of Benjamin Marshall on Tuesday, 3rd May, 2022, the Superintendent said to himself that he could have done without this politically-sensitive case just a few months before his retirement, but he had to carry on leading the teams.

It was on his orders that Commander Zandowski and Inspector Marceau requested a biographical summary from the US Embassy in France on Wednesday, 4th May, in order to find out slightly more about Benjamin Marshall, the victim. Thanks to this document, which they received within twenty-four hours, they perused the following information:

"BENJAMIN MARSHALL: American national, born in Washington on 9th November 1989, 1.85 m, light brown to blond hair, always cut very short, brown eyes.

Great-grandson of General Marshall, the US Secretary of State who initiated the Marshall Plan to help European countries recover economically after the Second World War. His father was a diplomat and his mother a translator at the State Department. The youngest of five, his two older brothers and two older sisters all worked at the State Department, or in the armed forces, or in the American intelligence services.

Breaking with the family tradition, he wanted to become a journalist, but in order to conform to that tradition, between the ages of seventeen and twenty-two, he underwent five years of training at West Point, the most prestigious of American military academies, from which he graduated with the rank of sub-lieutenant in the US Army. Then, perfectly bilingual in French and English, and finally feeling empowered to choose his career path, he went straight into the second year at the Paris Political Sciences Institute, in 2011, to study until the fifth year. After graduating in 2015, he joined the journalists' training school, where he studied his future profession from 2015 to 2017, while working as an intern in various French national newspapers.

At the end of his eleven years of higher education, not wishing to return to the United States because of the conflict between him and some members of his family over his choice of career, which they felt did not live up to their reputation in American diplomatic circles, he decided to become a freelance press correspondent in Paris for various American newspapers. For personal reasons, he specialised in investigative journalism.

On the day he was murdered, he was thirty-two and a half and had been working as a journalist for five years. His first investigation focused on Emmanuel Macron's attainment of the Presidency of the French Republic in the spring of 2017.

Subject to further information, these are the biographical details that the Embassy of the United States of America in France is able to provide you with, on Thursday, 5th May, 2022, for this American national."

On the same day, the Commander and the Inspector went to Benjamin Marshall's home in Rue Daguerre to carry out a neighbourhood investigation among the residents of his building and local shopkeepers, and to conduct a police search in the presence of two witnesses. They heard little from the first ones, apart from the fact that he left his home every morning at 8 a.m. to go to the scene of a report or to interview people mentioned in his articles. According to his next-door neighbours, he sometimes went out again in the evening to enjoy the rich cultural life of Paris, either for work or for private reasons.

The day before, after running his name through the police files, the two investigators had learned that Benjamin Marshall had lodged a complaint to his local police station two months earlier. The complaint related to the burglary of his flat and the theft of his digital devices, which had taken place one evening when he had gone out to the theatre. As the investigation had not produced any tangible leads, the police did not expect to find a great deal of information relating to his journalistic investigations when they searched his home.

Nevertheless, as a good professional, Benjamin Marshall had copied his old investigations, as well as the documents on which his in-progress articles were based, onto an online server, which enabled him to recover them on his new computer after the burglary.

Thanks to this precaution, the investigators were able to find all the stories he had written since the start of his career, in 2017, as well as those he was working on at the time of his death. They<were able to see that in 2017, in addition to Emmanuel Macron's accession to the Presidency of the French Republic, Benjamin Marshall had interviewed Thomas Pesquet on his return to earth on 2nd June, to illustrate a story on the six months he had spent in space.

That year, after attending the 14th-July parade, he had also investigated the resignation of the Chief of Staff of the French Armed Forces on 19th July, as well as the inauguration of a historical museum on the First World War by the French and German Presidents on 10th November, in Haut-Rhin department.

In 2018, he had written articles on the national tribute paid to Colonel Beltrame on 28th March, the entry into *The Pantheon* of Simone and Antoine Veil on 1st July and the Nobel Prize in Physics awarded jointly to a Frenchman, an American and a Canadian for their work on lasers on 2nd October. In November, he had produced a long article on the centenary of the armistice of the First World War, which had been commemorated in France in the presence of eighty-four Heads of State and Government, meeting in Paris at the invitation of President Macron, as well as on the first edition of the *Paris Peace Forum*, held from 11th to 13th November. In December, he had kept up with the actions of the Gilets jaunes and, especially, the damage done to *The Arc de Triomphe*.

In 2019, in May, he had reported on the fire at *Notre-Dame de Paris*, and in July, on the death of Vincent Lambert and the debate brought about by his situation: *should the treatment of a person in a vegetative state be stopped, even if he is not at the end of his life?* At the end of September, he had written a portrait of President Chirac, who died on 26th September. In December, he had written an article on the measures taken at the *Grenelle* summit to combat violence against women, the control being included in the French Penal Code and a bill being passed to introduce an anti-abuse bracelet for violent spouses and ex-spouses.

In 2020, he had written articles on the implementation of containment in the spring, as well as on the *Ségur de la santé*, a series of consultations with stakeholders in the healthcare system that ran from 25th May to 10th July. In the autumn, he had reported on the Nobel Prize in Chemistry awarded jointly on 7th October to two female researchers, one French and one American for molecular scissors, a technique for extracting one DNA sequence and replacing it with another. He had also written an article about the murder of the history teacher Samuel Paty.

In December, he had written a portrait of former President Valéry Giscard d'Estaing, who died earlier that month.

In 2021, on 5th May, he had published an article on the bicentenary of the death of Napoleon I. In August, he had reported on the withdrawal of the French army from Afghanistan and, in September, on the recall by France of its ambassadors from Australia and the United States, following the cancellation of the contract for the purchase of French submarines by Australia in favour of the Americans.

From 9th to 13th November, he had covered the official visit to France of Kamala Harris, the Vice-President of the United States, and on 30th November, he had written an article on the entry into *The Pantheon* of Joséphine Baker, the Franco-American actress and resistance fighter.

In 2022, before he was murdered, Benjamin Marshall was investigating work-related deaths on *The Grand Paris* building site, which was being launched in preparation for the 2024 Olympic Games, as well as management problems and breaches of medical ethics at the French subsidiary of a private American laboratory.

In addition to these articles, during the police search, Yanaël Marceau and Cédric Zandowski found around a hundred business cards at the journalist's home, which had undoubtedly been given to him by his professional contacts during his various reporting assignments.

As they went through them one by one, they were surprised to find one mentioning Lauriane Emans as a freelance writer. They immediately made the connection with the victim of the Soufflot Street case, who had occupied them five years earlier, and wondered how this quiet person, whom they had learned had moved to the Occitanie region in the spring of 2018, could possibly know Benjamin Marshall.

Using the contact details on the card, they decided to call her to make an appointment to hear her as a witness in the case. Although the Judicial Police Officers offered to interview her immediately at her home in Tombe-Issoire Street, in order to find out what she had done over the past five years and how she had known Benjamin Marshall, Lauriane Emans told them that she feared for her life since his murder and that she could not easily be absent from work during the week. The meeting was therefore set for Saturday, 7th May, at a hotel in the fourteenth district, not far from her home, where she could easily get in her wheelchair, without having to take time off work and without arousing suspicions in the case she was under surveillance on the orders of those behind the murder.

Given the length of the testimony she had to give, Lauriane Emans advised the Commander and the Inspector to make themselves available for the weekend.

These two investigators could not possibly imagine the turn their investigation would take after hearing this key witness.

Chapter 4

Lauriane Emans,
a key witness

Saturday 7th and Sunday 8th May 2022,
Hearing of Lauriane Emans
in a hotel near Tombe-Issoire Street
Paris 14th District.

T HAT WEEK, Commander Zandowski and Inspector Marceau went to a hotel in the Fourteenth District, in plain clothes and in an unmarked car, as discreetly as possible to protect their witness. After renting a meeting room, they welcomed Lauriane Emans. She was to give them her testimony about her relationship with Benjamin Marshall. The minutes of this hearing mention the following exchanges:

<u>HEARING OF LAURIANE EMANS BY JUDICIAL POLICE OFFICERS CEDRIC ZANDOWSKI AND YANAEL MARCEAU, ON SATURDAY, 7th AND SUNDAY, 8th MAY 2022, AT A HOTEL IN THE 14th DISTRICT</u>

JPOs: Lauriane Emans, can you tell us about events in your personal and professional life since February 2018, when we came to interview you at Cochin Hospital, as part of the Soufflot Street case?

Lauriane Emans: I was discharged from hospital in mid-February, just a few days after you came to interview me. In mid-March, after organising my move, I left Paris to begin my convalescence, both physical and psychological, in the Occitanie region. This lasted two and a half years, during which time I was treated by a private psychiatrist. Towards the end of this therapy, he advised me to resocialise professionally, which for him meant integrating myself with colleagues. To this end, he put me in touch with one of his friends, who had studied pharmacy at the Faculty of Sciences in Toulouse while he himself was studying medicine there. As this doctor of pharmacy had become Director of the French subsidiary of an American laboratory of international stature, my psychiatrist thought that, as an employee of this company, I could transcribe its most strategically important meetings.

Not without reluctance, and after much discussion with him, I finally accepted the idea of returning to Paris, where I moved into a flat on Tombe-Issoire Street in September 2020. That's when I started my permanent contract at the laboratory, which is located in a building on Maine Avenue and is so close to my home that I can get there in my electric wheelchair without having to depend on anyone else.

JPOs: How and in what circumstances did you come to know Benjamin Marshall?

Lauriane Emans: We met in January 2021 at the Literary Prize for Young Francophone Authors ceremony, organised by a well-known American platform in Paris. Having developed a self-publishing activity for detective novels during my convalescence, I published my first book there in January 2020 and, having been selected by the jury, I was invited to compete for this prize for 2021. As the platform is American, in order to give visibility to this ceremony and to the winning authors, its managers usually invite all the American press correspondents present in the capital to attend. This is how Benjamin Marshall and I came to meet and exchange business cards.

JPOs: Following this initial contact, did you meet up with him again at a later date?

Lauriane Emans: Between this ceremony, which took place in January 2021, and the Christmas holidays of 2021–2022, in other words, for eleven months, we had no contact. However, I know that during this period he wrote articles in the newspapers for which he was a correspondent in Paris about my detective novel whose American English translation I had published on the platform in September. The latter had sent a few copies, as a press release, to the American journalists who had attended the awards ceremony nine months earlier.

Having read these articles, I had been touched by the journalist's interest in my work as an author. When I felt the need to make public a number of shortcomings that I had observed during my work in the laboratory, I thought for a long time about who might be interested in receiving such sensitive information. After going through all my personal and professional contacts, I thought again of Benjamin Marshall, some of whose articles I had had the opportunity to read in the American press, in addition to those devoted to my book. So I knew that he carried out fairly in-depth investigations on rather original subjects, which set him apart from his colleagues. As he was an American citizen and correspondent in Europe for various American newspapers, I thought that the history of the laboratory, whose head office is based in New York, might be of interest to him. So I decided to tell him about all the problems I had seen at the laboratory.

JPOs: How did you reconnect with Benjamin Marshall?

Lauriane Emans: In order to contact him as discreetly as possible, I wanted to avoid the usual electronic exchanges, as well as meeting him in a café close to our respective homes. Knowing that his postal address was mentioned on the business card he had given me at the ceremony, at the end of December 2021, I sent him a handwritten letter by post to ask him if he would agree to communicate with me via a dead-letter box. I had previously created an email address specifically for our correspondence. If he agreed in principle, I suggested to him that I leave messages in the *Drafts* folder of this address in the morning between 8 a.m. and 1 a.m. to which he could reply, if he wanted clarification or to ask me some questions, between 1 p.m. and 10 p.m. by leaving messages in the same folder. In this way, since our exchanges did not leave the server hosting this specific email address, there was no risk of them ending up on the server hosting mine, nor on the server hosting Benjamin Marshall's email address. As they did not circulate on the Internet from an outgoing mail server to an incoming mail server, they could not be intercepted by anyone. As an investigative journalist dealing with sometimes sensitive subjects, I think he must have been used to doing this: he never replied to me that these were the methods of terrorists and he quickly accepted the principle of this type of exchange. So it began in the last week of December 2021.

JPOs: Between the end of your conversation and his murder, were you aware that he had been burgled and that his laptop had been stolen at the same time? Aren't you worried that someone might be able to trace back to you by analysing its contents?

Lauriane Emans: No, I didn't know that Benjamin Marshall had been robbed shortly before his death, as our exchanges were limited to the last week of 2021. I hadn't heard from him since. Given that he was very keen to protect his sources, I think he might have taken the precaution of deleting the browsing history on his old computer before it was stolen, so that no one could discover our mailbox. In any case, I hope so, so that his killers can't trace it back to me. If that were not the case, I am risking my life every time I leave my flat!

JPOs: In your opinion, what could have been the trigger for his burglary and the disappearance of his digital media?

Lauriane Emans: At the end of our discussions about the laboratory, he told me that he had to ask the laboratory for its version of the story I had told him, in order to assure the credibility of his investigation. So I think that between the beginning of the year and the burglary he was the victim of, he might have contacted the company's management to give it the opportunity to talk about the facts that implicated it. Not knowing exactly the extent or nature of the information Benjamin Marshall had about it, the company might have been able to monitor his comings and goings and taken advantage of his absence in the evening to order the burglary of his flat and the theft of his digital tools. After my own experience of working for this company, such a scenario does not seem improbable to me.

JPOs: From what you know about the latter, Benjamin Marshall's request to the laboratory could have been the trigger for his burglary, but could it have also been the motive for his murder, two months later?

Lauriane Emans: I think that at the stage he had reached in his investigations, Benjamin Marshall might have gathered a great deal of information about this laboratory through our exchanges, as well as through the contacts he might have had with people who are familiar with the world of health economics. Given that this information was likely not only to cause the company to lose a lot of money, but also to give it a bad reputation from which it could never have recovered, I wouldn't be surprised if, in the panic of a crisis, a radical decision had been made.

JPOs: Are you telling us that the information you gave Benjamin Marshall about this laboratory could have led to its managers commissioning his murder?

Lauriane Emans: Absolutely. Those are my exact words.

JPOs: Was the information you had so sensitive for the reputation and the expansion of this laboratory?

Lauriane Emans: Absolutely.

JPOs: How did you have access to it?

Lauriane Emans: I had access to this information thanks to the meetings of the Steering Committee and of the Works Council, which I was responsible for transcribing after having attended them along with the other speakers. Even though I didn't speak, I had ears to hear and eyes to see the exchanges, some of which sometimes seemed surreal. Once these meetings had been transcribed, I had their minutes, which I had written myself from the recordings, and needless to say, by dint of transcribing and rereading them, I knew them by heart!

JPOs: Of course, but didn't you sign a confidentiality clause when you validated your contract at the time of your recruitment?

Lauriane Emans: Absolutely. When I was hired in September 2020, I signed a clause to the effect that I committed myself not to divulge the content of these meetings to anyone outside the company. However, given all the vexations and humiliations I suffered within the working environment, in 2021, it was the last straw. From the end of last year onwards, I felt I was no longer bound by any duty of loyalty to my employer and, at the same time, by my voice of confidentiality.

After careful consideration, I took advantage of the calm of the festive season to contact Benjamin Marshall, to tell him about the many events I had had to face throughout 2021 within the context of my work. At the same time, I also told him about the various breaches of medical ethics that the laboratory was guilty of. Even though they didn't concern me directly, I felt it was my duty to report them in order to avoid a health scandal involving minor patients.

This is the very long story I am about to tell you.

Chapter 5

A compromised integration

*Testimony of Lauriane Emans heard by JPOs
about professional events that occurred
between September 2020 and December 2020.*

MY NAME IS Lauriane Emans and I am at the centre of this whole story.

From now on and for several chapters, I am going to tell you about the incriminating facts I revealed during my hearing with JPOs Cédric Zandowski and Yanaël Marceau on 7th and 8th May 2022, as part of their investigation into the murder of Benjamin Marshall. They also form the basis of the story I told to the Toulouse psychiatrist Arnaud Wagram in September 2023.

After convalescing in the Occitanie region, at the end of August 2020, I moved back to Paris, where on Tuesday, 1st September I started work, on a permanent contract, as a meeting transcriber at the French subsidiary of a private American laboratory specialising in research and development in the field of innovative health technologies. On the recommendation of my psychiatrist, the Director had recruited me without any difficulty, given my law degree and the freelance work I had practised by transcribing meetings during my last two years at university and during my convalescence.

Having lost his wife in the attacks that had plunged Paris into mourning in 2015, and having been informed by my psychiatrist of the Soufflot Street case, at the time of this interview, this manager had shown me a certain empathy with regard to the ordeals I had been through during this affair. He assured me of his benevolence, his full and complete confidence in my intellectual abilities, and his interest in the work I would be doing for his company. From then on, we would meet once a week at Steering Committee meetings and once a month at Work Council meetings. According to my job description, I was required to attend these meetings as an observer, in order to follow the main points, the digital audio recordings being used as a basis for the transcriptions of the detailed minutes that I was responsible for making.

At first, all was well, and I thought I was finally going to be able to embrace life on the bright side, after all the events I had encountered during my years as a young adult.

In the staff organisation chart, I was placed under the authority of the Human Resources Manager, who was forty years old and had been in the job for ten years. As soon as I arrived, which had been planned for two months, I realised that my department manager had done nothing to help me integrate into the department, even less into the company overall. Every person I met asked me, with the contemptuous air of someone who thought I didn't belong there, who I was and what I was doing on the executive floor where my office was. However, it wouldn't have been very complicated for the Human Resources Manager to send an email to all the employees, and especially to the managers I was going to meet during the Steering Committee meetings, as well as to the staff representatives I was going to meet during the Works Council meetings, to tell them that the management was recruiting a person with reduced mobility and to explain to them what my job was going to consist of.

By the end of that first week, which had only lasted four days, I was already exhausted from having to answer the same questions at least twenty times. To keep my hopes up for the future, I told myself that these questions would certainly diminish over time, once the staff on the directors' floor had got used to seeing me wandering around the premises in my wheelchair.

The following week, I began to hear rumours in the corridors that I was the Director's niece, or his mistress, depending on the versions. I wondered who could have been spreading such things, although I was careful not to answer them so as not to fuel them.

September and October passed like that, in a climate which I couldn't say was really hostile towards me, but which I couldn't say was really benevolent either. Instead, I had the feeling that I was facing one of those latent, muted attacks, the origin of which I had difficulty identifying, which prevented me from responding as I should have done. Trying hard to produce irreproachable transcriptions, I thought that the situation could only improve with time, once my skills and the usefulness of my work had been fully appreciated.

As I wasn't in a position to respond to this unhealthy climate for the time being, due to a lack of information, I decided to show the greatest indifference towards it, even though, inwardly, I was beginning to feel tormented about this integration that had never really taken place: I wondered if this failure wasn't going to bring into question a recruitment process to which I had already committed a great deal of effort.

The events that followed did nothing to improve my situation: on 29th October, the President of the French Republic announced the implementation of a second national lockdown, which was to last until 14th December. Teleworking measures were imposed, particularly for people whose health was at risk from the Covid-19 epidemic. Because of my pre-existing brain damage, the consequences of which if I caught the virus no member of the medical profession was able to tell me, I found myself under lockdown at my home, just one and a half kilometres from the company's head office.

Having previously worked as a transcriber from home for five years, even though it wasn't for the same company, I didn't take offence at this situation and I adapted to it without any problems. However, this was not the case for all the managers: during this period, the Human Resources Manager asked me to install a piece of software on my computer to record my working time, even though this one could have been assessed by right-clicking to access the details of the properties of each transcription file, including its editing time corresponding to my working time.

At the end of this lockdown, on Tuesday, 15th December, I was ordered to go back to work in the office, like the other employees. During the week leading up to the Christmas holidays, a large number of employees seemed to be enthusiastic about a tradition that had originated in North America and was to take place before the holidays: the organisation of a secret santa. In order to comply with this tradition, each employee had to give a gift to another employee in the company and receive one in return, with the aim of strengthening the bond of the teams and of the work group. As far as I was concerned, I hadn't been given a sufficiently long or high-quality period of integration, which would have enabled me to form friendships with colleagues. Consequently, I couldn't see who I could have offered a gift to and whom I could have received one from in return. I wasn't going to do so with the Director, as benevolent as he was towards me; otherwise I risked being seen as someone in the pay of management, which would add to the rumours that were already circulating on the subject!

I therefore asked the Human Resources Manager for permission to withdraw from this practice, at least for the year 2020, because of the lockdown. On the one hand, the latter had prevented me from developing sufficiently close relationships with my colleagues, so I didn't feel I was in a position to offer a gift to anyone. Furthermore, as a matter of principle, I always refused to receive anything from my professional partners other than remuneration commensurate with my work. On the other hand, there were only four days left before the Christmas holidays, and because of the physiotherapy sessions I had to do three times a week after my working day, I didn't have enough time to find a suitable gift online and to receive it by the postal service before the holidays.

A dialogue ensued between the Human Resources Manager and me on this subject:

The HRM: You're really making no effort to fit in at this company!

Me: I did try at the beginning, but the lockdown that lasted a month and a half didn't help and I wasn't the person who had decided that, it was the President of the Republic!

The HRM: That's no reason to neglect your obligations!

Me: Yes, but I don't know anyone in the company intimately enough to whom I could give a gift, and in those circumstances I would be embarrassed to receive one myself.

The HRM: All you have to do is draw lots from the list of employees. As you work under my authority, you can easily access this list, can't you?

Me: Yes, but if I draw someone I don't know, I can't see myself giving him/her a present nor asking him/her to give me one in return.

The HRM: So what do you want to do about this situation?

Me: I don't know. Perhaps you could exempt me from this obligation for this year. After all, it's not in my employment contract. So you can't force me to take part in it.

The HRM: Of course, but it's customary to do it.

Me: Yes, it's a custom, but the latter isn't written in the French Employment Code nor in my contract. As far as my presence in the company is concerned, I come to work to earn my living and to feel useful to the society, not to make myself look good in front of management, nor to make friends with my colleagues, and even less so after what happened last September.

The HRM: What happened last September that I wouldn't have known about?

Me: You didn't tell anyone I was coming and everyone looked at me strangely, as if I didn't belong on the executive floor. Under these conditions, I had to answer the same questions twenty times to justify my presence on the premises. Yet it would have been very simple to send an email to all the staff members to tell them what my role was with regard to the management team and to ask them to give me the warmest welcome, as you should do for any newly recruited employee, shouldn't you?

The HRM: Ms Emans, I'm your line manager and as a recent recruit, as you say, it's not up to you to tell me what I should or shouldn't do within the framework of my work!

Me: Admittedly, as your subordinate, it's not up to me to tell you, but if certain shortcomings are having a negative impact on my working conditions, it's up to me to tell you, knowing that you have the opportunity to remedy the situation. Everyone talks about secret santa as a way of reinforcing the bond within the work group, but before you foster this, isn't it your duty to foster the integration of recent recruits, and even more so that of a person with reduced mobility whose presence on the management floor you knew very well would be the subject of speculation by everyone?

The HRM: The fact that you were recruited by the Director, and that your trial period is over, doesn't mean you can take the liberty of doing anything you like: if you continue in this tone, you are going to receive a warning for insolence and this will appear in your file as a disciplinary sanction.

Me: It's not because I was recruited by the Director that you were obliged to do nothing to facilitate my integration. I take note of your threats of disciplinary action, and I realise that it's impossible to discuss anything with you without you mentioning your hierarchical power at every turn! That's why I prefer leaving it at that for today. I wish you a Merry Christmas, though!

The discussion between the Human Resources Manager and me on the subject of the secret santa came to an end that day, and this collective event took place on Friday, 18th December, from 3 p.m. to 6 p.m. From 3 p.m. to 4:45 p.m., I refrained from taking part, staying in my office on the pretext that I had a transcription to finish before I went on Christmas holidays, and nobody asked me anything. At 4:45 p.m., as planned, an ambulance driver came to pick me up and take me to Montparnasse Street, where I had an appointment at 5 p.m., at a physiotherapist's office for my third physiotherapy session of the week.

I couldn't imagine how I would later pay dearly for my stubborn refusal to take part in the secret santa.

Chapter 6

A literary prize is something to celebrate, but not for everyone

Testimony of Lauriane Emans
heard by the JPOs
about events that occurred
in her professional and personal life
in January and February 2021.

O N MONDAY, 4ᵀᴴ JANUARY 2021, at the end of the Christmas holidays, I went back to work at the laboratory, hoping that the New Year would wipe out the old grudges between myself and the Human Resources Manager that had built up over the last quarter of 2020. However, something quite unexpected was about to happen to generate further tension between us.

On Monday, 18th January, I was informed by email that I was to receive the literary prize awarded to young authors for the detective novel *A Case For The Paris Police*, which I had published in January 2020, a year earlier, and in which I had recounted the case of the same name of which I had been the victim, in 2017. In 2019, while I was still undergoing psychotherapy to recover from this traumatic event, my psychiatrist, Arnaud Wagram, knowing my propensity for writing detective novels, had advised me to write about it in novel form. According to him, this exercise should have helped me to become aware of my schizoid personality disorder and should have helped to alleviate it. So I had written this book in 2019 and published it on a famous American self-publishing platform, without suspecting for a moment that I was going to receive an award for having successfully completed this project.

In the email I received on 18th January, it was stated that I was to go to a hotel in the Sixteenth District of Paris, where the prize-giving ceremony was to take place, on Thursday, 28th from 6 p.m. However, on Thursday evening and Tuesday evening, I was supposed to stay at work until 7:53 p.m., to make up for the hours I couldn't work in the late afternoon on Monday, Wednesday and Friday. On those days, instead of leaving at 6 p.m., I had to leave the office at 4:45 p.m. and arrive at 5 p.m. at Montparnasse Street, where I had to carry out my three weekly physiotherapy sessions. When I was hired, it was agreed with the HRM that I would work until almost 8 p.m. on Tuesday and Thursday evenings to make up for the time not worked during those three working days. As soon as I heard about the award, I asked my manager for permission to leave at 5 p.m. on Thursday, 28th January, so that I could get to the ceremony on time. Our exchange on this subject went something like this:

Me: Good morning, Madam. I need an exceptional leave on Thursday, 28th January, starting at 5 p.m., which would mean leaving the office at that time instead of at 7:53 p.m. as usual.

The HRM: What is the reason for your request?

Me: I am due to attend a literary prize-giving ceremony in the Sixteenth District, starting at 6 p.m.

The HRM: Can't this ceremony take place without you?

Me: No, not really.

The HRM: Why is that? Do you think you're essential?

Me: No, I don't think so, but I have to receive one of the prizes that are to be awarded at this ceremony. If I don't go, it wouldn't reflect well on the jury who decided to award it to me.

The HRM: I didn't know you were a writer.

Me: I didn't know myself until I became one. I started this activity at a time when I wasn't yet working for the laboratory.

The HRM: You didn't mention it on your CV. Are you hiding it?

Me: It's not really an activity, more a hobby that I do in my spare time while other people are doing sports or cultural activities at the weekend or on holiday.

The HRM: It's a bit strange that you should receive an award for an activity that you only consider to be a hobby!

Me: Very few authors make a living from their writing! That's why I regard writing more as a hobby than a professional activity. In fact, I neither sought nor asked to receive this prize, but now that it's been awarded to me, I have to find a way of making myself available so that I can attend the presentation ceremony.

The HRM: The problem is that on Thursday evening, you are supposed to recover the time you take to go to your physiotherapy sessions, during three other late afternoons falling on working days.

Me: Indeed, but I propose that I come to work on the Saturday morning before, on 23rd January, from 9 a.m. to 11:53 a.m., in order to do the two and a half hours of work that I won't be able to do on Thursday, 28th in the late afternoon.

The HRM: After your absence from the secret santa, you're certainly not missing an opportunity to draw attention to yourself!

Me: Believe me, that's not my intention!

The HRM: Admittedly, but if I begin giving absence permissions to one person, I'm going to have to do the same for every employee. In that case, what's the point of collective working hours? You have to respect them, in the same way as the other employees, and without asking me for time off at every turn!

Me: For the few months I've been working in your department, I don't think I have ever asked you for absence permissions at every turn, and I don't intend to do so in the future either. I'm only asking you for this favour so that I can deal with what we might call exceptional circumstances: I'm not going to receive a literary prize every day. It usually only happens once in a lifetime, and it would be a real shame if I weren't able to attend this ceremony!

The HRM: It would also be a real shame if you didn't do your job that day! So I'm refusing to give you this permission. You will have to endeavour to be represented at the ceremony!

Me: Who do you want to represent me there? I don't have any family in Paris and I haven't lived there long enough to know anyone I could trust to represent me.

The HRM: I don't care about your personal problems! We don't feel sorry for ourselves in this office! Please get back to work and stop wasting my time with your writer's moaning!

Me: That's not moaning!

The HRM: Perhaps, but this activity has nothing to do with the one you carry out for the laboratory, and I hope you don't do it during your working hours!

Me: Of course not! Who do you think I am? Do you think I'm dishonest when I offered to come to work on a Saturday morning to make up for the missing hours?

The HRM: I know what you have offered me, but in view of the other employees, I can't do you this favour.

That was the end of our discussion on the subject, and as I was unable to reach an agreement with the Human Resources Manager, I sent an email to the Director to explain the situation. Very happy that I was singled out by this famous platform for my work as an author, he gave me the permission to be absent from the office from 5 p.m., on Thursday, 28th January, without even asking me to come to work on the previous Saturday morning to carry out the missing hours.

In order to get the message across to the staff, he wrote an article on the subject, which he asked the communication department to include in the next publication of the company's internal newspaper. So, at the end of January, everyone knew that *"Lauriane Emans, who is responsible for transcribing the minutes of the Steering Committee meetings and those of the Works Council meetings, has won a literary prize for a detective novel she had published on a famous American platform in 2020."* In a fitting tribute to this award, the Director emphasised how *"well deserved it was"* and congratulated himself on having recruited me from among his employees, who are so *"intelligent, innovative, creative and adapted to today's constantly changing world."*

As the Director chairs the Works Council, the institution which brings together management and staff representatives, he asked me whether, as part of the social and cultural activities of the latter, I might be interested in giving a talk on the subject of my book within the company. Faced with such a request, I couldn't but accept, even if I didn't feel very comfortable when I had to speak in public.

The Director then asked his assistant to organise this talk in the amphitheatre where it was customary to gather all the staff when the management had an oral communication to make to them. He also arranged for an article on the subject to be published in the company's internal newspaper and on Thursday,

18th February 2021, from 6 p.m. to 8 p.m. instead of working to make up for my time off at the end of the day, I explained the origins of my writing activity, as well as the story of my book, to the three hundred people who had come to listen to me out of the six hundred employees of the laboratory's Paris subsidiary. At the end of my talk, half of the people in the room asked me to sign my book, which they had bought online, and I was very touched by this sudden interest in my writing.

So, although my integration went badly because of the reluctance of the Human Resources Manager to organise it as it should have been, during my first three months of work in the lab, the zeal shown by the Director in relation to my literary prize contributed greatly to make me known and recognised by the other employees. Knowing that my work as an author had nothing to do with that of the laboratory, I wasn't asking for much, but I had to admit that from the end of January onwards, and even more so from the time of the talk, no one asked me who I was or why I was on the management floor when I met someone I didn't know in the corridors.

Thanks to the Director, my request for absence permission for the late afternoon of 28th January had been granted, and at the same time I had overcome the difficulties associated with my failed integration.

However, as the Human Resources Manager had not said her last word, one day I was going to pay very dearly for all the publicity surrounding my literary prize.

Chapter 7

Sabotage

*Testimony of Lauriane Emans
heard by the JPOs
about professional events occurring
from February to July 2021.*

FOLLOWING all the publicity surrounding my literary prize carried out by the Director, which had the effect of giving it even greater weight, from February 2021 the Human Resources Manager, who didn't like me before, decided to make my life a living hell. To this end, she indulged in various acts of sabotage aimed either at preventing me from doing my job properly, or at preventing me from working at all.

On several occasions, she brought forward the dates of meetings of the Steering Committee and those of the Works Council without informing me, even though we belonged to the same department and I was supposed to attend to them. At these meetings, everyone present was surprised that I wasn't there, while I didn't even know they were taking place. So I continued to transcribe the previous meeting, in my office, on the same floor where the Steering Committee or the Works Council was being held.

These last-minute reschedulings also had the disadvantage of disrupting the schedules of the staff representatives due to attend the Works Council, as well as those of the fifteen or so departmental heads and members of management due to attend the Steering Committee, including the Director. This situation led to a number of malfunctionings at the time, but the Human Resources Manager didn't care: intent on getting me to leave the company and knowing that, as a disabled employee protected by the Labour Code, she couldn't dismiss me without the authorisation of the Labour Inspector, she did everything in her power to get me to leave, even if it meant engineering problematic situations between the participants that could only be solved through her.

When these meetings were over, the Human Resources Manager was responsible for recovering the original recording and giving me a copy from which I was to transcribe the minutes, but from February onwards I received barely audible audio files from her. Because of my hypersensitive hearing, I avoided using headphones as much as possible, usually contenting myself with using high-fidelity speakers. However, given the poor audio quality of the recordings sent to me by the Human Resources Manager, I had to use the earpieces of my mobile phone in order to hear the speakers clearly, which made me twice as tired as usual while doing the same amount of work.

Another technique used by the Human Resources Manager to make my work more difficult was to give me recordings with constant background noise, which made it difficult to hear what the speakers were saying. During the meeting, for example, she would regularly open the door of the room in which it was taking place, while several people were talking in the corridor near the door. Similarly, from April onwards, when the weather was fine, she would open the window of the meeting room a few centimetres, while the children from the nearby primary school are outside during break, which had the effect of saturating the recording with high-pitched sounds and making it more difficult to understand what the various speakers were saying. When she couldn't make an excuse to open the door or the window, she deliberately made noises near the recorder, handling papers or pens which she dropped noisily back onto the table, creating unpleasant sounds on the audio files.

When I transcribed meetings recorded in this way, I had to distinguish between the words of the various speakers and the extraneous noise. This only increased the amount of time I had to devote to transcribing each meeting, and on several occasions I had to transcribe a meeting when I hadn't yet finished transcribing the previous one. I told myself that, if this situation carried on, I might be heading straight for a burnout. To avoid such an outcome, I decided to ask for a discussion with the Human Resources Manager, which led to the following exchange:

Me: Good morning. I asked for this discussion to talk to you about the meetings you pass on to me for transcription. I have noticed recently that the recordings are inaudible and regularly polluted with noise, which doesn't make my work any easier. Would it be possible for you to increase the volume and keep the door and the window closed during the meetings?

The HRM: Do you think I open the door and the window for pleasure, during the meetings?

Me: As the meeting room is air-conditioned, I don't really understand why you regularly open either the door or the window. I have also noticed that you open the door when there are people in the corridor and the window when the school children are outside during break. I find that a bit surprising.

The HRM: Are you accusing me of deliberately spoiling the recordings?

Me: No, of course not, but the background noise generated by these situations contributes greatly to the deterioration of my working conditions, by increasing the transcription time I have to devote to each meeting.

The HRM: As a professional meeting transcriber, you need to be able to transcribe under any circumstances without your working time or the quality of your work being affected.

Me: Perhaps, but, like Michael Scofield, I suffer from a latent inhibition deficit that doesn't allow me to distinguish, when I hear different noises, between those that are essential and those that are secondary, which makes it very difficult for me to transcribe meetings with background noise. That's why I'm asking you if you can avoid giving me the task of transcribing meetings with background noise of any kind.

The HRM: I don't know who Michael Scofield is. He must be another of your novel characters, I imagine! But here, we are in real life: you haven't been recruited to write novels, so you have to adapt to the constraints of the company you work for!

Me: I certainly understand your point of view, in principle, but at the same time, I am not a machine and I don't see why I should have to put up with such a deterioration in my working conditions!

The HRM: You can always complain to the staff representatives!

That was the end of our conversation, and needless to say, the recordings I received, from that day on, didn't get any better.

Finally, to conclude on the subject of the deterioration in my working conditions, I have to tell you that, from February 2021 onwards, the lift in the lab broke down regularly, and when I arrived in the morning, I was often unable to get to my office on the tenth floor of the building in my wheelchair.

Faced with this situation, which was incongruous, to say the least, I had no choice but to return home, either to continue my transcriptions in progress after transferring, from home, my work files from my work computer to my home computer, or to record the meetings remotely myself. To do this, I had to log on to *Teams* to capture the meeting as a live stream, but as I didn't have administrator rights to the company's *Teams* account, recording the meetings remotely proved very complex to set up from home.

In order to achieve this, I had to read up on how to do it and, once I had learnt the theory, I had to replace the audio drivers on my personal computer, initially graded for its operating system, with those for its motherboard and carry out all sorts of other technical adjustments to my audio settings. I managed to recover the recordings without mishap each time the lift broke down, and no one worried about whether this was technically possible without having administrator rights on *Teams*.

While I was subjected to actions deliberately intended to disrupt my working conditions, I came to think that the indifference of the hierarchy faced with the difficulties encountered by employees was also a form of sabotage of their work in Enterprise 2.0.

I was far from imagining of that I hadn't yet reached the end of the hell that my Human Resources Manager had in store for me.

Chapter 8

Pierre Dobriac, the friend found again

December 2023,

Arnaud Wagram's recounting of what happened

in the personal life of Lauriane Emans

from February to August 2021.

WHEN Lauriane Emans returned to my office for a consultation in September 2023, she told me about the events following her literary prize, which took place in her personal life between February and August 2021.

In February 2021, thanks to the notoriety generated by this award, she received an email from Pierre Dobriac, the ambulance driver who had discovered the crime scene and saved her life in September 2017 during the Soufflot Street case. The latter had disappeared just four days after performing this emergency rescue and no one had heard from him since. So investigators and his former colleagues had thought he was dead. Lauriane Emans had also thought that he must have died, or that he had disappeared voluntarily, given the control to which he seemed to have been subjected within the couple he formed with Mrs Z, his partner at the time. In fact, it was as a tribute to this ambulance driver, whom she considered as a friend, that she had decided to write this story, after I had suggested to her, during her therapy, that she should write a fictionalised recounting of these traumatic events.

In January 2021, having heard about this literary prize in the newspapers, Pierre Dobriac had recognised the author's name as that of his former patient. He had bought her book and, after retrieving the email address mentioned in it, he had contacted her. He had then explained to her that he had been kidnapped on Thursday, 7th September 2017 and held hostage until the end of February 2018 by people he believed to be hired men in the pay of Mrs Z. According to him, at the time, the latter, who had previously shown a marked tendency towards paranoid jealousy of the female patients he worked with, wouldn't have put up with the media hype generated by the Soufflot Street case. So she would have immediately taken retaliatory measures against him in order to discourage him from forming friendships with his patients, while avoiding getting her own hands dirty. So, on the very day that Pierre Dobriac had disappeared, she had found a way to flee to the United States and take up a permanent post in New York at the pharmaceutical company's head office, where she had previously been head of sales in France. This subterfuge had prevented her from having to return to France to answer for her actions before the courts, with regard to a situation that had been immediately considered by the investigators of the Third Judicial Police Department as a worrying disappearance.

At the end of February 2018, Mrs Z had judged that the punishment had lasted long enough, and Pierre Dobriac was released by his captors after six months of confinement in a place that he was unable to locate, except that it must have been in the Paris region. Informed at home that he was wanted by the criminal investigation department for his disappearance, he had contacted the investigators of the Third Judicial Police Department. However, as he had been unable to provide them with sufficiently relevant information to enable them to prosecute his captors and prove Mrs Z's involvement in his abduction and confinement, the case had been closed without further action.

Pierre Dobriac had therefore had to relearn how to live, with the feelings of shame and humiliation he felt, following this ordeal, the aim of which had been to make him lose all self-esteem.

A fortnight after his release, he had gone to Lauriane Emans' home to find out what had become of her since the attack on 4th September 2017. As she had moved to the Occitanie region a few days before he went to her home, he had only been able to note that her name no longer appeared on the intercom and on what had previously been her letterbox. So they had just missed each other, and as they hadn't previously exchanged their email addresses, he couldn't contact her that way either. Faced with this dead end, which had added to his sadness at the time, he had only been able to give up.

He had then tried to re-establish his daily routine. To this end, he had returned to live alone in his flat on Delambre Street, in the Fourteenth District. After undergoing six months of physical and psychological rehabilitation, not wishing to become an ambulance driver again, he had trained to become a private security and cybersecurity agent from September 2018 to January 2020. At the end of this training, he had set up his own business, and because of the threats to cybersecurity, which had multiplied during the various lockdowns, his business had quickly flourished.

This was the information exchanged by Pierre Dobriac and Lauriane Emans by email and when they met again in Paris in February 2021: after agreeing by phone to celebrate their reunion, they decided to spend some time together over a meal in a restaurant. During the latter, they had each explained in detail their respective setbacks, and had been moved by the ordeals suffered by the other, especially Lauriane, who felt both responsible for the imprisoning of her friend and indebted to the man who had saved her life three and a half years earlier.

From that day on, they had been united by an unbreakable friendship, and they had met each other several times between February and July 2021, either to share a meal in a restaurant, or to go to the cinema or the theatre, or to attend classical music concerts that they both loved. During these various meetings, each confided their torments to the other, while respecting the silences that sometimes came naturally in their conversation when an event from their tragic past resurfaced.

In August 2021, both of them being off work, they decided to go on a fortnight's holiday together to a famous seaside resort on the Atlantic coast. Of course, Lauriane, in her wheelchair, couldn't enjoy a swim in the ocean, but the cafés and restaurants along the seafront welcomed her at their tables, so she could take in the fresh air and admire the landscape. Early in the morning, when the weather remained springlike, Pierre and Lauriane sometimes went for long walks on the paths along the coast. Everyone took them for lovers, but given their respective painful pasts, they didn't really care how others looked at them: they took full advantage of these moments of calm and complicity, knowing that no professional or private constraints were going to disrupt their schedule.

During their stay, emboldened by this pleasant setting and by their mutual friendship, Lauriane decided to confide in Pierre about the various annoyances that she suffered from her Human Resources Manager at the laboratory, not knowing whether she should describe them as careless omission or malevolence. Even though he was almost twice her age, and despite his life experience and recent training in the safety of people and property, Pierre was unable to give her a precise answer on this point. However, outraged by what he considered to be an inadmissible behaviour in a professional context, he advised Lauriane to complain to the Director. Nevertheless, as the latter was responsible for her recruitment, she didn't want to bother him with her personal problems with the Human Resources Manager.

As their conversation on this subject progressed, Lauriane also told Pierre that she wanted to leave the company as soon as possible to protect herself from the various acts of sabotage that she was being subjected to, which she considered to be moral harassment. However, he advised her not to give up in the face of adversity, and told her that she had to fight for her right to better working conditions. He went on to suggest that she should "*discuss the matter with a journalist if the situation worsens after the summer break.*" According to him, "*the fact of making malpractice public could sometimes contribute towards a certain awareness among the members of a group previously subject to inertia caused by the force of habit, whether these members are suffering from them, or whether they are themselves the source of them.*"

As this advice was, in her opinion, at the root of Benjamin Marshall's murder, for which she felt partly responsible, in September 2023, I asked Lauriane Emans why she hadn't contacted me, by email, at that time, to explain the situation in which she was struggling with her Human Resources Manager. Knowing her previous fragility, due both to her schizoid personality and her overdeveloped emotional and sensory sensitivity, I would have assessed her level of suffering and advised her to resign in order to safeguard her mental health. She replied that, feeling indebted to the Director and to me for her job at the laboratory, she hadn't wanted to bother us with her problems.

So it was through this strange linking of circumstances that Lauriane Emans, Pierre Dobriac and I thought we were, to varying degrees and more or less directly, involved in the murder of the only American journalist to be shot dead on French soil, Benjamin Marshall.

Chapter 9

Little Adrien,
a stigmatised schoolboy

*Yanaël Marceau's recounting
of events occurring in his personal life,
from September 2021 to the end of October 2021.*

I N SEPTEMBER 2021, after having completed four years' service as a police lieutenant, I was promoted to the rank of police inspector in the criminal investigation department, in accordance with the normal promotion procedure. I then continued my career as a Judicial Police Officer in the Third Judicial Police Department, where I was subordinate to the orders of my friend and commander Cédric Zandowski. The team being reduced to two investigators, I became the group's procedural officer. A lieutenant was due to be recruited to strengthen our team, but the hierarchy didn't seem to be in any hurry to fulfil this task. So we were swamped with work, due to the sudden effect of this reduction in manpower.

At that time, my son Adrien, who was also the son of Camille Huguenot, the criminal psychologist who had been sharing my life since we met in 2017 during the investigation into the *Soufflot Street case*, started nursery school. Being three years old, he was our first child and the fruit of our love affair. We had decided to name him Adrien, in memory of my twin brother, who had the same first name. Brown-haired and blue-eyed like me, my son looked exactly like my twin and when I looked at him, I couldn't help thinking of the latter. He died before my very eyes from a stray bullet in Marseille, where we lived with our parents when we were ten. Not a day went by that I didn't think about him. In fact, I think I can say that my vocation as a criminal investigation officer gradually came to me as a result of this trauma. Unconsciously, when I was a teenager, at the time when I was making my career choices, I had decided to turn to a profession that would enable me to make up for injustices, as if, by doing so, I would be able to do justice to my brother who died too soon. Of course, at the end of my seven years of study, when I was appointed to the Third Judicial Police Department, in 2017, I had quickly realised that the reality was quite different. To this day, it hasn't made me bitter, and I still practice my job with the same enthusiasm and passion.

Coming back to our son Adrien, very soon after he was born, our whole family affectionately nicknamed him "*Little Adrien*" to distinguish him from Adrien, my twin, whose memory we sometimes called to mind by imagining what he might have become if he had had the chance to live through his adolescence and go on to adulthood.

So in September 2021, Little Adrien started in the infant class at one of the nursery schools located in the Seventeenth District, near our flat. Just when we thought everything was going well for him, on Friday, 22nd October 2021, the eve of the All Saints' holiday, Camille and I were summoned by the headteacher of the school for a meeting, the purpose of which had not been made known to us in advance. Moreover, the teacher and the assistant responsible for the infant section also attended.

On this occasion, these three people told us with great conviction that our son was disrupting the class by impulsively answering his teacher's questions without permission. They also told us that, because of an attention deficit resulting either from restless behaviour or constant daydreaming, they were obliged to repeat instructions to him several times before he decided to follow them. In short, according to them, our son, affected by Attention Deficit Hyperactivity Disorder (ADHD), had become unmanageable.

We were obviously stunned by this revelation, all the more so as, since the start of the school year, we hadn't noticed anything unusual in his behaviour when he was with us. At the time, I was so busy working in our minimalist team that I often left early for the Third Judicial Police Department to start my shift at 8 a.m., and just as often returned home late, usually around 9 p.m. So when I left the flat in the morning, our son had barely got up and was still in a sleepy limbo, and at the time I returned in the evening he was already in bed. Even though I never failed to stop by his room to place a kiss on his sleeping forehead, I could only notice that I was seeing him less and less.

When the school's educational team gave us this piece of information, I wondered, because of a certain ambivalence, how to handle the situation. On the one hand, I didn't accept the fact that my son would be stigmatised as disabled for life, from the age of three, but on the other hand, I didn't think I was in the best position to call into question the word of the teaching staff who were close to him all day long. Camille, my partner, who had studied psychology up to master's degree before her training period with the police, was in a better position than me to assess the relevance of this opinion, and from the outset, she challenged this diagnosis, which seemed to her completely wrong. She was willing to admit that, since starting nursery school, Little Adrien had sometimes been tired, grumpy and restless at the end of the day, but, having spent the first three years of his life cocooned with a nursery assistant who looked after only three children at a time, how could it have been otherwise?

Armed with this certainty, Camille told the educational team that, as our son had been at the school for only a month and three weeks, he might need extra time to adapt to the demands of being integrated into a group of twenty or so pupils who were each one just as young and perhaps just as affected as he was by this new situation. None of her arguments seemed to convince the headteacher and her two subordinates, and we were therefore ordered to have our Little Adrien undergo a neuropsychological assessment as soon as possible, in order to evaluate the extent of the ADHD he might suffer from, according to the statements of these three people who considered themselves to be well informed on the subject.

At the time, we were too shocked by this intransigent attitude towards us to react. We left the school with a feeling of unease and not really knowing whether we were going to follow these instructions in the weeks to come. The two of us even debated whether it would be better to move our son to another school rather than leave him in an educational environment where he was now stigmatised.

During the All Saints' weekend, when we had managed to get our two families together at our home, which rarely happened, each of his four grandparents gave their opinion. In the end, some of them contradicting the recommendations of the others and each of them showing themselves to be both sceptical and undecided about the solution to be adopted in such a situation, we were not helped by the respective opinions of our relatives.

At the end of that All Saints' weekend, Camille and I agreed on what seemed to us the wisest possible decision, even if, with the passing of time, it may seem like an easy one: we decided to continue sending our Little Adrien to the same school, in the hope that giving him a few extra weeks to adapt to the nursery school would put a definitive end to his restlessness and his trouble concentrating.

After all, having been born in July 2018, he was only three years and four months old: he had plenty of time to be labelled as dysfunctional in a world where children are no longer allowed to grow up at their own pace!

Chapter 10

Prison Break at the lab

Testimony of Lauriane Emans
heard by the JPOs
on a professional event occurred
on Tuesday 7th December 2021.

AFTER the summer holidays and during the autumn of 2021, I carried on going to the lab to transcribe the meetings of the Steering Committee and the Works Council. The Human Resources Manager continued to sabotage me, as that was her usual trick, but I hadn't reached the new depths of my anguish yet. That was exactly what happened to me on Tuesday, 7th December, from 7 :53 p.m.: as I was about to leave the building, after having done my two hours fifty three minutes overtime, in compensation for the days when I had to leave the lab at 4 :45 p.m., I noticed that the door of my office was closed. As this lock had been activated automatically by the building's electronic locking system, I couldn't deactivate it by any means whatsoever. So instead of making my way quietly back to my home, where I usually arrived at around 8:10 p.m., after having spent a quarter of an hour using my electric wheelchair on pavements and pedestrian crossings, I found myself stuck in my office on the tenth floor of the building.

Faced with this situation, which was incongruous, to say the least, I decided to call up the private company responsible for providing the security of the building during the hours when the lab was closed, in order to have my office door remotely reopened. I was then answered by a temporary employee who told me that he wasn't empowered to remotely deactivate the building's general lock, which was a prerequisite for reopening my office door electronically.

Undaunted, knowing that I had downloaded the *My Security* application on my tablet, I selected the *I'm a victim* option and was immediately put in touch with the nearest police rescue unit to my location, the one linked to the fourteenth district police station. I explained my situation to the officer who answered my call: "*I'm a person with reduced mobility in an electric wheelchair. I work on the tenth floor of a building on Maine Avenue and the door of my office has been automatically closed by the activation of the building's electronic locking system, so I can't get out.*"

The agent asked me if any of the company's managers had the codes to deactivate this system. I replied that, as far as I knew, some of them did have this information, but that on the day in question, instead of leaving the office at 8 p.m., they had all left the building exceptionally, at 6:30 p.m., to go to *Roissy-Charles-de-Gaulle* airport. Once there, they were due at around 7:45 p.m. to board the 8:25 p.m. flight to Australia arriving on Wednesday evening, Paris time. On the following Thursday and Friday, they were due to attend the laboratory's annual world congress, held this year in Melbourne.

As it wasn't yet 8:25 p.m., but only 8 p.m., the agent advised me to try and reach one of these executives before the plane took off. So I tried to get in touch with the Human Resources Manager and with the Director, but I went straight to their answering machine, which left my situation unchanged. Nevertheless, I left a message to alert them to the situation and waited until 8:25 p.m. for one of them to call me back. However, as they had probably switched their phones to aeroplane mode during boarding, shortly before my call, neither of them realised, before the plane took off, that they had received an extremely serious message. As a result, no one called me back to give me the unlocking codes that would have allowed me to leave my office and the building. So I called the emergency police again to tell the agent, who had already answered me, that I hadn't been able to contact anyone before the plane took off and that I was still trapped in my office on the tenth floor of the building.

As the flight to Australia was due to last twenty-one hours and the automatic opening of the building couldn't be released by the security company until 8 the next morning, I couldn't decently wait that long for someone to come and rescue me. The agent therefore decided to dispatch a police rescue squad to secure the perimeter, while awaiting the arrival of the first rescue team from the nearest rescue station, whom he had warned as a precaution while I had been trying to contact my superiors.

Unable to deactivate the electronic lock on the building's doors, the rescuers decided to get me out of the building through my office window. Concerning this, I realised that as the windows on the upper floors were sealed off to prevent suicides, my office window could only be opened a few centimetres from the inside and could not be opened from the outside. The rescuers therefore decided to deploy the aerial platform at the end of the main ladder to cut out the glass from the outside, using extrication equipment. As this was a triple-glazed window, they had to work on it for at least an hour before they were able to cut through it. As soon as the first crack was made in the wall, the building's intruder alarm began to sound continuously and at high volume, alarming everyone in the neighbourhood for an hour, after which it had been programmed to stop automatically.

As for me, at 9:30 p.m., I was still locked up in my office, which now had no window, while it was dark and it was December, which didn't help to maintain the temperature in the room. The first rescuers brought me something to eat and a survival blanket while I was waiting for the next stage of the operation.

I had to get my wheelchair out in the fireman's aerial platform. I got on it, manoeuvring it just as I would have done to get into a lift, except that I was twenty-five metres off the ground and I suffered from vertigo. My wheelchair and I weighed a total of one hundred and eighty kilos, I asked the rescuers beforehand if the aerial platform could bear that much weight, as well as that of the two of them who came with me throughout the manoeuvre. In the end, we weren't far from the four hundred kilos conforming to the regulation, but as the total of our respective weights didn't exceed this limit, it wasn't necessary to call for the perilous environment response group helicopter to winch up my wheelchair. That was fortunate: I had got enough of a fright for the day!

At the end of this incredible operation, the rescuers would have liked to take me to the nearest hospital for observation. However, realising that they weren't going to know what to do with my electric wheelchair while I would have been transported in their vehicle, it was quickly decided that their doctor, who was on site, should examine me. After making sure that I wasn't injured and that my blood pressure was low enough not to require any special monitoring, the doctor gave permission to two other rescuers to get me back home nearby, each one walking on either side of the wheelchair.

As for my office, it was now a gaping hole, open to bad weather. While I was waiting for the glass to be replaced, I ended the year 2021 by taking a sick leave from Wednesday, 8th December to Friday, 17th December. Then, from Saturday, 18th December 2021 to Monday, 3rd January 2022, I went on Christmas holiday. So, in order to preserve my mental health, I tried to completely break away from the lab until the start of the new year in January, that is to say for three and a half weeks.

This was the situation, unexpected, to say the least, that the company's executives discovered on their return from the congress. I hoped for their sake that they had had a good time during the few days they had spent in Australia. In 2022, the time would come to establish who was responsible for such a fiasco, someone who would have to answer for themselves before the staff representatives, the Labour Inspector, the police and the courts.

ADHD and video games, care for Adrien

Yanaël Marceau's recounting of persona events that occurred during the 2021–2022 Christmas holidays.

A T THE START of the All Saints' Day holidays, our Little Adrien returned to the same nursery school, Camille, his mum and I having decided not to move him to another educational establishment in order to avoid perturbing him. We hoped that his hyperactivity would diminish over time once he had adapted to life in a group. Nevertheless, on Friday, 17th December 2021, we were summoned once again by the headteacher, who came with the teacher and the assistant responsible for the class in which our son was provided with schooling.

As we had not followed up the interview of 22nd October, during which we had been told to have him undergo a neuropsychological assessment for suspicion of ADHD, the school returned to the attack. Since then, having decided to give our child time to grow up and required by our respective professional obligations, we had found neither the motivation nor the availability to have him undergo a consultation with a competent practitioner in the field.

When we told the headteacher that we had serious doubts about her diagnosis, she called us *"unworthy parents"*, which was the last straw for a police officer and a criminal psychologist! To top it all, she threatened to refuse to provide our son with schooling after the Christmas holidays if we took no action in this respect during that period. We felt that this person was becoming too intrusive in our lives, making diagnoses for which she had no qualifications. However, for the well-being of our Little Adrien and to avoid making the situation worse, we told her that we would deal with the problem during the holidays.

In this situation which was uncomfortable, to say the least, the fact that Camille had studied advanced psychology constituted an asset for us: she spent the Christmas holidays looking for a place for our son in the consultation schedules of all the child psychiatrists in Paris capable of carrying out such an assessment, which turned out to be very specific. However, during the festive season, either the medical offices were closed altogether, or the only offices still open were unable to see a new patient for several months.

Confronted with the carelessness of the medical system, as the days went by, we were wondering whether we weren't going to have to change our son's school at the start of the new school year in January. At Christmas dinner, which we spent with friends and family, and at New Year's Eve dinner, to which we had invited a few friends, the unseemliness of our situation amazed everyone. Once again, everyone had their own comment to make and at the end, no one agreed with anyone else about the solution to adopt. So for the first weekend of 2022, we found ourselves more alone than ever, with our anguishes as young parents.

At the height of our dismay, Camille decided to call one of her old university friends with whom she had kept in touch on a more or less regular basis and who worked as a child psychologist at the Necker Hospital in the Fifteenth District. On this occasion, the latter mentioned an experimental programme, developed by an American laboratory, to treat ADHD by having patients play very specific video games. According to her, the stimuli used during this therapy were likely to reduce the distractibility of the brains of children and teenagers suffering from this disorder, and therefore improve their concentration.

Since the 2000s, we had heard so much about the harmful effects of video games on the immature brains of children and adolescents that we found it hard to believe that they were authorised to treat attention deficit disorder, especially for patients as young as our son. So we asked her about it, and the psychologist assured us that it was safe to try. Moreover, if we wanted Adrien to take part in this experimental programme for which places were limited, we had to decide quickly. So, between the headteacher of the school, who threatened to refuse to provide him with schooling if he didn't follow a care procedure, and the small number of places allocated by the hospital for this treatment, we really had the impression of being caught between a rock and a hard place!

To give our son the best possible chances of success, we had to commit to take him to his rehabilitation sessions three times a week for a year. As the Necker Hospital was situated on the opposite side of the city from our home, we would have to travel across Paris at rush hour for each session, except on Wednesdays, which was a considerable constraint on our already overloaded schedules. Usually, Adrien stayed at the nursery until 6 p.m., when Camille picked him up, and on Wednesdays he was looked after at our home by a babysitter. We therefore had to ask her to come with our son to his therapy sessions on Monday evenings and Friday evenings after school, as well as on Wednesday afternoons.

Finally, this treatment, not yet validated by the health authorities, was not reimbursed by the health insurance scheme. Before giving our consent for Adrien to be included in this clinical trial, we were warned that we would have to pay the sum of ten thousand euros, immediately. This exorbitant sum was to be used, on the one hand, to pay for the hospital care, which was itself responsible for paying the few practitioners qualified to supervise this treatment and, on the other hand, for the Parisian Hospital Group rights to use the protocol under licence from the American laboratory that had developed it. When we saw ourselves obliged to incur such an expense, we had the impression that our son was going to be selected for a private preparatory school to integrate medical studies or the Parisian school of political sciences. But no, he was only three and a half and already under the pressure of a society in which only the best-brainwashed and most successful members manage to adapt: in this increasingly crazy world, there was no space for daydreaming or distraction, even for young children!

As a result, at the end of our Christmas holidays, our son was able to start the new school year in January in his usual nursery school and the headteacher, having learned that we had enrolled him in a care procedure, no longer considered it a good idea to refuse to provide him with schooling. Camille and I were relieved to have resolved this problem, which had seemed insoluble at the start of the holidays.

At the time, I didn't yet know that a news item I would be investigating in 2022 would give me the opportunity to discover the existence of numerous malfunctions within this American laboratory, some of which would have an impact on my personal life.

Chapter 12

Staggering revelations

Testimony of Lauriane Emans
heard by the JPOs,
on personal events occurring
during the 2021-2022 Christmas holidays.

THE DAY AFTER my misadventure, which was incredible, to say the least, the national newspapers and all-news channels picked up on this news, photographing or filming from Maine Avenue the now gaping hole in what used to be my office window.

On his return from Australia, the Director of the lab, having been informed of these events, asked for my permission to come to my home, where I was on sick leave, to give me some comfort after the ordeal I had just been through. As I felt no animosity towards him, I agreed to see him and we discussed my situation over a cup of coffee, which I offered him as a courtesy. Taking advantage of his attentive listening, away from the indiscreet ears of the office, I told him in detail all the interpersonal difficulties I had had to face, due to the behaviour of the Human Resources Manager, since I had been recruited in September 2020 and even more so since I had received my literary prize at the end of January 2021. He regretted that I hadn't told him about this earlier, and that he had had to wait for something tragic to happen to assess the reality of the situation.

As the legal representative of the legal entity that was the company, he was responsible for ensuring the health and safety of his employees when they were at work, an area in which there had just been a major failure. As such, the lab risked a very heavy sentence, as well as a sharp increase in the monthly social security contribution it paid on each salary, in respect of accidents at work and occupational illnesses, should I decide to take it to the industrial tribunal, the court responsible for dealing with workplace disputes.

To avoid going to such an extent and, above all, to avoid the lab being the subject of bad publicity, the Director offered me compensation in the form of a settlement worth fifty thousand euros. Not having the courage either to take legal action or to look for another job, I accepted this proposal, not knowing whether it came from the Director alone, or whether the Board of Directors had approved it. If it had not, I thought that I could wait a long time to receive the fifty thousand euros I had been promised! For the time being, as this was an agreement in principle, no document validating this transaction had been submitted for my signature.

At the end of my sick leave, I took my Christmas holidays and because of Covid-19, which was still rampant in enclosed spaces, I preferred to avoid travelling by the high-speed train. So instead of spending the holidays with my family, I stayed in Paris. My psychiatrist would say that my schizoid personality disorder didn't naturally incline me towards family gatherings. Be that as it may, I stayed in Paris during that period, and I began to feel anxious about coming back to work in the lab in January.

My friend, Pierre Dobriac, whom I had informed of these events at the start of my sick leave, spent the next four weekends with me to comfort me. This gave us the opportunity to resume our discussion, about the malfunctions I was having to deal with in the lab, where we had left them the previous summer when we had spent a fortnight's holiday together. He was adamant that if I wanted things to change, I should discuss the situation with &a journalist.

As for me, after such a succession of unfortunate events and despite the financial compensation I had been promised, my loyalty to my employer having reached its limit, I felt that I had been released from my confidentiality agreement. At the end of the weekend of 18th and 19th December, I started looking around among my acquaintances to see who I could talk to about the particular situation I had been increasingly subjected to since I had been recruited, but also about what I had seen and heard at meetings of the Steering Committee and of the Works Council.

Going through the business cards I had collected since my return to Paris, I came across Benjamin Marshall's card. Knowing that he was an American citizen and an investigative journalist for various newspapers in his home country, I thought he might be interested in the story of the lab, which was based in New York.

On Monday, 20th December, I wrote to him at his home, reminding him that we had met almost a year earlier at the award ceremony for the literary prize for young French-speaking authors, organised by a well-known American platform. I then briefly explained that I wanted to talk to him about the American laboratory I was working for. Finally, I explained that, in order to ensure greater discretion in our exchanges, I had created a dead-letter box where I could leave messages in the morning, to which he could reply in the afternoon or evening. If he wished, we could also chat live, which presupposed that we were connected to the mailbox server at the same time. So I gave him the web address, the username and the password so that he could connect to it, and I asked him to reply to me on the mailbox to let me know if he agreed to collect sensitive information in this way.

By the time Benjamin Marshall received my letter and the Christmas holidays were over, he replied to me using this communication channel on Monday, 27ᵗʰ December. We spent the last week of the year exchanging the following messages.

Benjamin Marshall: Good afternoon, Ms Emans. I received your letter. That's why I'm getting in touch with you, as you requested. As an investigative journalist, I am, of course, interested in any information that could be used in a journalistic investigation, especially if it relates to an American company, as readers of the newspapers for which I am a correspondent may be very interested in such information. From what I have read in the French newspapers, I understand that you recently had to leave your office at the very least in a rather bizarre way, after being locked in for several hours. Can you confirm it to me?

Lauriane Emans: Good afternoon, Mr Marshall. Thank you for your interest in my situation at the lab. I can confirm that on Tuesday, 7ᵗʰ December, I found myself locked in my office from 6 :30 p.m. to 10 p.m., even though I didn't realise it until 7 :53 p.m., when I wanted to leave and go home at the end of my day's work. The rest is history.

Benjamin Marshall: How did you end up in such a perilous situation?

Lauriane Emans: You should ask the person who activated the general electronic locking system for the building's doors, bearing in mind that it couldn't be deactivated before 8 a.m. the next morning, when the first employees arrive.

Benjamin Marshall: Was there no one on the site capable of deactivating this system?

Lauriane Emans: Only a few managers in the company would have been able to deactivate it, but as they were boarding the plane for Australia when I tried to contact them, no one went back to me before the plane took off. The rest is history.

Benjamin Marshall: In your letter, you more or less suggested that the illegal confinement might have been intentional. Do you have any idea who might be behind it and why?

Lauriane Emans: To answer your question, I have to briefly describe my career at the lab: I was recruited by the Director in September 2020. My job consists in transcribing the minutes of meetings of the Steering Committee and the Works Council. I work under the Human Resources Director. Now, as soon as I arrived, she immediately took a dislike to me, although I'm not sure why.

Benjamin Marshall: Can you give me some typical examples of this situation?

Lauriane Emans: When I arrived at the lab, the Human Resources manager hadn't told anyone that a disabled employee in a wheelchair was now on the payroll to transcribe the company's most important meetings, which completely ruined my integration. Then she refused to grant me a leave of absence to let me attend the literary prize-giving ceremony, where we met.

Since learning of this honour, she has decided to make my life, at the lab, a living hell, making me transcribe badly-recorded or even inaudible meetings, which has the effect of worsening my working conditions and extending my working hours. Sometimes she even goes so far as to bring forward meeting dates at the last minute without telling me, so that I can't attend them.

Finally, since last February, the lift has often broken down and, as nobody has gone to the trouble of letting me know, I have discovered this disaster on arriving at the office in the morning. As a result, I am unable to access the upper floors and have to return home to record the meetings from my personal computer without having administrator rights on *Teams*, which is no mean feat.

Benjamin Marshall: I understand your dismay. In your opinion, what could be the reasons for the Human Resources Manager's behaviour towards you?

Lauriane Emans: There could be several: first of all, as she is very concerned with appearances, it's possible that she doesn't appreciate people in wheelchairs because of the image of incompleteness, or weakness, that she believes reflects negatively on her in comparison with her capabilities as an able-bodied person. I understand that, faced with a disabled person in a wheelchair, some people wonder what they would do if they found themselves in the same situation, which can sometimes lead them to become aggressive. However, as a manager trained in the recruitment of disabled employees, the Human Resources Manager should be able to put her prejudices aside. Secondly, as all recruitment usually goes through her, I think she never accepted the fact that I was recruited directly by the Director, without him ever asking for her opinion on the matter. It's also possible that she thinks I am a spy in her department, working for him, although that is a bit far-fetched.

Finally, she regularly criticises me for coming to work only to do my job and never trying to establish more personal contact with her or my colleagues over the coffee machine. So, under the pretext of getting to know the employees better, she often asks them questions that have nothing to do with work: for example, in order to demonstrate a false complicity with me, she sometimes asks me if I have a boyfriend. Refusing to play along with her, I answer that she only has to read my CV to find out!

In the same vein, every time I come back from holiday, she systematically asks me if I have been on holiday and I answer her equally systematically: *"No, I haven't been on holiday."* As this

Human Resources Manager loves to show off *her* "*superb husband, superb children and superb holidays*", she doesn't understand what pleasure I can find in staying in Paris during my holidays, when, if I wanted to, I could very easily have a change of scene. So she thinks I am telling lies, or hiding something, when I tell her I haven't gone on holiday. In fact, because of the constraints of transporting my electric wheelchair, I limit my movements to a strict minimum, spending most of my free time reading or writing detective novels at home, which I have been careful not to explain to her, believing that it is none of her business.

Finally, I have also noticed that she has shown more animosity towards me since I received my literary prize. At the time, I think she only saw me as a person with a disability, who was inevitably missing something, instead of seeing me as the whole person I am before I am a person with a disability. She would never have imagined that I could receive an award for any activity whatsoever. That is why when I had to talk to her about receiving this literary prize, in order to ask her for a leave of absence, she seemed offended by the fact that I have an ability that she herself doesn't possess, which only accentuated her already significant jealousy of me.

Benjamin Marshall: Do you plan to take legal action against the lab for the illegal confinement you suffered in your office?

Lauriane Emans: No, I am not planning to take legal action against the lab, especially as I am still working there and don't have the courage at the moment to fight to find another job elsewhere. To be completely honest, I have to tell you that, following this accident at work, the Director offered me a compensation of fifty thousand euros. I accepted this settlement in principle, but to date I have not received any document validating this agreement.

Benjamin Marshall: Could you tell me about this company's corporate purpose, legal structure, sources of funding and number of employees?

Lauriane Emans: This laboratory, based in New York, specialises in research and development in innovative healthcare technologies. It is financed by private shareholders, who are individuals or legal entities of American nationality. Its French subsidiary, where I work, has six hundred employees. A third of them are medical representatives linked with the French sales department, most of whom work regionally to promote the brand's products to hospitals and private practitioners. The management has also set up subsidiaries in Canada, in Japan, in Australia and in Germany.

Benjamin Marshall: Do you know what their research is about?

Lauriane Emans: The lab's researchers have been actively working on the discovery of an innovative antiviral drug for several years, and not just since Covid first appeared. They are also conducting clinical trials to find a treatment that uses video games to treat children and teenagers suffering from ADHD. This topic is often called to mind by staff representatives at the Works Council, the Director and the Medical Director putting pressure on the researchers to market the treatment as quickly as possible, despite the fact that it is experimental and that its efficacy has not been proven yet. I even think that the researchers are sceptical about it, improvements in the behaviour of minor ADHD patients not being sufficiently convincing yet for them to hope to market such a treatment in the long-term.

Benjamin Marshall: You mean to say that the Medical Department is trying to obtain permission to market a treatment that it knows to be ineffective, doesn't you?

Lauriane Emans: I don't know if it is possible to talk about ineffectiveness. In any case, to date, the real effectiveness of such a treatment has never been proven in significant group trials.

Benjamin Marshall: How do you think the Medical Department would go about obtaining marketing permission for a treatment with limited medical benefit?

Lauriane Emans: Either by providing falsified test results to the supervisory authorities, or by trying to corrupt the agents of the bodies responsible for granting these permissions. However, I have no proof of what I am saying. This is just how I feel when the subject comes up at the meetings I attend. In my opinion, given the extent of the ADHD market in our time, the financial stakes are too high for anyone not to give in to the temptation to tinker with the results of these experiments, or to bribe certain people in a way that is favourable to the lab.

Benjamin Marshall: You are making some very serious accusations against this company, aren't you?

Lauriane Emans: These are not really accusations, but rather suspicions based on my feelings, which only a police investigation could back up. If you take up my comments, I would ask you not to mention the fact that you obtained them through me.

Benjamin Marshall: Of course, don't worry: I will respect the confidentiality of my sources, but in order to strengthen the credibility of my investigations, I am obliged to interview the lab about its position on all the points you have just made.

Lauriane Emans: I have no problem with that, as long as you guarantee my anonymity. Please let me know when your article is published. Goodbye, Mr Marshall.

Benjamin Marshall: Goodbye, Ms Emans.

My first virtual exchanges with Benjamin Marshall ended on the evening of 2nd January 2022, the date on which we agreed to contact each other again if I had any new information to share with him, or if he had any further details to ask me, while he was writing his journalistic investigation about the lab.

I had no idea at the time that, with his assassination five months later on 3rd May 2022, those first virtual exchanges would also be the last.

Three investigations, one case file

July 2022,
Yanaël Marceau's recounting
of the investigations carried out
from January to June 2022.

T HROUGHOUT THE WEEKEND of Saturday, 7th and Sunday, 8th May 2022, as part of the investigation into the murder of Benjamin Marshall, Commander Cédric Zandowski and I had collected a lengthy testimony from Lauriane Emans about various non-functional aspects she claimed to have been aware of at the American laboratory where she had been working since she was hired in September 2020.

On this occasion, our witness revealed management problems, of which she felt she was the direct victim, as well as breaches in medical ethics of which the laboratory would have been allegedly guilty with regard to minor patients. In support of her claims, she had provided us with the access codes to the dead-letter box on which she had exchanged messages on this subject with Benjamin Marshall during the Christmas holidays. At the end of her testimony, we therefore had both her oral statement and her written version of the facts, as she had told this journalist a few months earlier.

Provided with all this information, we searched the police files about this laboratory and discovered that, in January 2022, at an extraordinary meeting of the Works Council, the staff representatives had asked the Director to open an investigation about the illegal confinement Lauriane Emans had suffered, in order to determine how such an incident could have occurred. At the end of the latter, they had sent their report to the Labour Inspector regarding this situation, which they considered unacceptable in terms of working conditions. When the Labour Inspector had received their report, he had immediately referred the matter to the Public Prosecutor to ensure that such incidents were severely punished before the criminal court.

When the investigation into the murder of Benjamin Marshall began in May 2022, the Lauriane Emans part of the laboratory case was still under investigation. Moreover, the pace of the French justice system being what it is, the judicial police had not conducted any hearings on this subject yet. Noting that these two cases were closely related, because they were clearly linked, the public prosecutor, in his opening indictment, asked the examining magistrate to group together the two cases so that they could be dealt with, each in relation to the other, by the same judicial police officers.

And so, from mid-May, Commander Zandowski and I got found ourselves plunging into the case not only of Benjamin Marshall, but also that of Lauriane Emans, under the orders of the examining magistrate Bernard Lourmel who, four and a half years earlier, had investigated the Soufflot Street case. In addition to the illegal confinement of Lauriane Emans and the murder of Benjamin Marshall, we also had to investigate the lab's breaches of medical ethics, denounced by Benjamin Marshall in one of the yet-unpublished articles he had written before his death, and by Lauriane Emans during their discussions. We therefore had to tackle this investigation from three different angles.

For convenience of language, and when the distinction between these three aspects was not obvious, among ourselves we called this file "*The lab case.*"

The day after Benjamin Marshall's murder, at the beginning of May 2022, when we had glanced through police files, we had discovered that he had been burgled two months earlier, the purpose of the breaking-in having been to remove his work tools and documents. According to Lauriane Emans, he had been robbed because he had sought to obtain, in accordance with journalistic ethics, the laboratory's version of the breaches of medical ethics that she had previously told him about. Again, according to our witness, after the burglary, Benjamin Marshall would have returned to the attack regarding the laboratory. Thus, unable to silence this journalist, the latter would have ordered his murder to avoid exposing the irregularities of which he was guilty in the clinical trial using video games on the treatment of minors suffering from ADHD.

Provided with this information, from 9th May, Judge Lourmel gave us the priority of doing everything in our power to prevent a health scandal involving minor patients from developing, at least on French territory. We therefore decided to focus our investigation on this treatment, which the laboratory presented as innovative. To this end, during a search, we seized the minutes of the previous six months' Steering Committee meetings. On reading these documents, we discovered that the Director was putting enormous pressure on the Medical Director to ensure that the researchers supervised by the latter found an innovative ADHD treatment as quickly as possible.

We also seized the minutes of the Works Council, which is made up of the Director, the Financial Director, the Human Resources Manager and a staff representative from each of the company's departments. When we read these minutes, we learned that the latter regularly denounced, during these meetings, the pressure put on researchers by the Medical Director to find an innovative treatment for ADHD and Covid-19 as quickly as possible.

Our aim was therefore to check whether this pressure had led to any ethical breaches, and to this end we seized documents from the Medical Department relating to the treatment of ADHD using video games. From these we learned that, since January 2022, this clinical trial had been administered to a cohort of one thousand patients in bevery country in which the company had set up a subsidiary, as well as in the United States. In total, this clinical trial involved six thousand minor patients aged between three and eighteen, at a cost of ten thousand euros per patient in Europe and twelve thousand dollars in other countries. However, as this treatment had not yet been validated by national or continental health agencies, it was not reimbursed by health insurance systems, which meant that the cost was passed on to each family involved.

Secondly, each patient's medical sheet mentioned the progress that had been made after three months of therapy, carried out at a rate of three half-hour sessions per week. As this treatment was offered to children and teenagers of different ages, each of whom could have been suffering from different symptoms of ADHD for different lengths of time, it seemed fairly strange to us that the progress recorded in each patient was all at the same stage, without discrimination as to age, the nature of the symptoms or the known duration of the disorder. We didn't know whether this similarity of results was inherent to the way the trial protocol was conducted, or whether it was a trick designed to enable the laboratory to obtain the marketing permission for this treatment.

By this time, my own son, Adrien, had already had the latter for four months. As the results of this clinical trial were being transmitted to the lab in real time, when I was studying the documents, I found the evaluation form that the medical team at Necker Hospital had filled in for him. As far as I could make out, three months after Adrien had started his treatment, it mentioned encouraging progress for the first time, whereas the teaching staff at the nursery school told us that they had seen no improvement in his behaviour. According to the three people who looked after him at school, he was still just as restless, or daydreaming, or impulsive, depending on the day, and he still disrupted the class just as much, speaking up when he wasn't invited to and was always moving around.

As far as the form is concerned, as the procedural expert of our group, I was in a good position to know which documents were, or were not, included in the procedure, and, that day, I misused this position: in order to avoid having the investigation withdrawn, I stole my son's evaluation form, which, I admit, was not a very ethical behaviour. By doing this, I wanted to avoid the risk of the opposing party requesting that the procedure be cancelled on the grounds that I was too personally involved in the investigation and, as a result, that I lacked impartiality, a position the latter could always accuse me of, even if I tried to remain restrained in my analysis of the case.

Behind the scenes, specialists in judicial policing, who were assisting us with this investigation, called up the thousand French families involved in this treatment, whose results, mentioned on the patients' evaluation forms, did not seem to us to be guided by scientific rigour. During this remote hearing, each of them told us that after four months of treatment, their respective children had made little progress, unlike the information given on their assessment forms. In view of the cost of the treatment, some families were even considering joining their forces to defend their interests in a class action against the laboratory for fraud and aggravated deception.

When we had finished with this first part of *The Lab Case*, towards the end of May, Judge Lourmel asked us to investigate further the illegal confinement of Lauriane Emans in her office on Tuesday, 7th December 2021. To this end, we reviewed the minutes of the Works Council meetings seized during the police search. On this occasion, we noted that the Human Resources Manager, believing herself to be essential, had taken a certain ascendancy over the management team and had assigned herself the role of the person in charge of the building's safety, whereas she should have confined herself to managing the staff in her department, recruiting members of staff for all departments and ensuring that collective labour relations were well maintained. The latter included employee health and safety at work, a prerogative that falls under the employer's social responsibility in French companies.

On the other hand, the building's security was a matter for a private security company, which was responsible for ensuring that the building was inviolable outside working hours and for managing access to it during working hours, as well as opening it at 8 a.m. and closing it at 8 p.m. However, the staff representatives' investigation report stated that the Human Resources Manager had taken the responsibility for activating the door locking system at 6:30 p.m. on Tuesday, 7th December, while Lauriane Emans was still inside the building. Since those who commissioned the internal report did not comment on the nature of this act, it was left to the criminal investigation to determine whether it constituted negligence or pure malice. For the time being, the least that could be said was that the Human Resources Manager had, on that day, assumed without rights a prerogative that did not fall within her duties!

Pending the hearing of the people implicated in the facts set out above, we concentrated on the burglary and murder of Benjamin Marshall. As the autopsy on his body had not provided us with any convincing results as to the origin of the weapon with which he had been shot, Judge Lourmel asked us to carry out a personality investigation on each member of the management team, as well as of the laboratory's executives, a total of around twenty people. Our aim in doing this was to check whether one or more of them had a criminal record or links with organised crime. Finally, we studied the telephone records of the subsidiary's six hundred employees. At the end of these technical investigations, we found no link that could connect anyone to this short news item.

We did the same with the members of the building and public works companies responsible for the *Grand Paris* construction site in preparation for the 2024 Olympic Games. As Benjamin Marshall had investigated the work-related deaths that had occurred during the construction work, the judge had concluded that some of their directors or managers might have had an interest in silencing him before the publication of his article on the subject, in order to avoid seeing their reputation damaged. We found nothing suspicious on that score either.

These were the conclusions we sent to the examining magistrate at the end of July 2022. At the time, Commander Zandowski and I had no idea that the further investigation about Benjamin Marshall would turn out to be unexpected, to say the least.

Chapter 14

Behind appearances

Yanaël Marceau's recounting
of the events occurring
in his investigation
in September 2022.

O N MONDAY, 5th SEPTEMBER 2022, after a month's rest, which was very beneficial for both of us, Commander Zandowski and I resumed our investigations into the lab case, whose priority suddenly changed direction: whereas the Judge Lourmel had decided to investigate first and foremost the treatment of ADHD using video games, in order to avoid a health scandal involving minors, he received an email from his superiors, the Criminal Cases Management, which sounded more like an order than a suggestion. This told him that, in view of the French president's State visit to the United States from 30th November to 2nd December, the investigation into the murder of Benjamin Marshall absolutely had to be given priority forthwith.

The judge and his management then decided to add to our team a commander from the Criminal Squad, who would be in charge of this part of the case. From experience, we knew that when the Criminal Squad took charge of an investigation, the latter concerned either a sensitive field, or a particular personality, or one who was particularly exposed.

Nevertheless Commander Zandowski and I had not been idle on this case: in four months, we had carried out numerous investigations, but these had not really enabled us to find any clues that might lead us to a sleeping partner or an executor. For a while, we suspected the lab, or even the building and public works companies responsible for building the *Grand Paris* project. However, as no evidence was found to support this theory at that stage, it was necessary to look at the case from another angle.

As a result of this decision, things didn't drag on as long as they often do in the Civil Service: when my teammate and I arrived at the Third Judicial Police Department, the next morning, Superintendent Langlois introduced us to Commander Christophe Servallin, who was forty-five years old and had been assigned to the Criminal Squad for five years. In addition to his training as a criminal investigation officer, he also had a master's degree in cultural anthropology, which is why he had been asked to take charge of this case.

In the same way that Judge Lourmel had not been very happy to receive orders from his superiors regarding the investigation of this sensitive case, Commander Zandowski was not particularly delighted to be replaced as head of the group responsible for this investigation, but, since the reason of state demanded it, he too had to come to terms with it.

Once we had resolved to accept the situation, we decided to integrate Commander Servallin into the investigation about the murder of Benjamin Marshall without any fuss. To this end, Commander Zandowski and I reviewed for him all the information we had at our disposal: the victim's complaint about the burglary and the theft of his digital devices, the crime scene file, the forensic information gathered during the autopsy, the biographical note provided by the American embassy, the list and content of Benjamin Marshall's articles and working documents, his exchanges with Lauriane Emans, as well as the findings of our searches, personality and telephone investigations.

After studying Benjamin Marshall's biographical details and the articles he had written since the start of his career as an investigative journalist in 2017, Commander Servallin put forward an original hypothesis, to say the least: Benjamin Marshall's profile had been invented by the American secret services in order to establish the legend of an undercover agent in Europe. This meant that, since he set foot on the Old Continent in 2011, his official identity had been fictitious. It also meant that his status, successively as a student and a journalist, had merely been a cover enabling him to carry out intelligence activities on behalf of the United States in Europe, such as recruiting sources and gathering sensitive information in political, economic and strategic circles.

In support of this thesis, Commander Servallin gave us, as well as in the report he submitted to the examining magistrate forty-eight hours later, the following arguments:

"Benjamin Marshall's date of birth, 9 November 1989, corresponds to the day the Berlin Wall came down. It is not uncommon for the secret services responsible for developing a legend to give their undercover agents birthdates that, while fictitious, are historically symbolic of one side's victory over the other.

**Benjamin Marshall was sent to Europe after five years of training at the best American military academy, in line with the profile sought by the secret services when recruiting a field agent whose mission is to collaborate with human sources, or to infiltrate sensitive environments in foreign territory.*

**His studies at the Paris Political Sciences Institute and at the journalists' school were designed to give him the training he needed to cover as a journalist, while at the same time enabling* him to make contact with his fellow students, some of whom would go on to become influential, or be placed in strategic positions, a few years after completing their training. Studying at French civilian schools also enabled him to erase his overly military appearance and become a clandestine agent with the appearance of a civilian capable of blending into the mass of the population in which he would have to operate.

*The fact that he specialises in investigative journalism and has carried out numerous investigations linked to European political, economic and strategic circles gave him the ideal cover to infiltrate these circles without drawing attention to his activities as a spy.

*The date of his death, 3rd May, corresponds to the day of commemoration of freedom of the press, which turns out to be rather ironic when you look at his biography: given the large number of articles he wrote during the period in which he practised his cover as an investigative journalist, it is possible to suppose that he mistook his legend with the mission for which he had been sent to Europe in 2011 as a covert agent of the United States. This means that instead of carrying out the recruitment of human sources and intelligence gathering, he had given priority to his activity as a journalist.

This kind of split personality sometimes occurs when clandestine agents have been stationed in a foreign country for too long. The solution is therefore to pull them out of that territory and repatriate them to their country of origin, where they are then retrained in another department. However, in the case in point, given his degree of involvement in journalism, the American secret services certainly decided that Benjamin Marshall could not be rehired.

*Given the sensitive information relating to US policy to which he had access during his training at West Point and then, through his handling officer, during his clandestine activities in Europe, *the American secret services feared that, because of his split personality, he might reveal some of it in his articles. In these circumstances, having become unmanageable on the ground and unable to be recycled in his home country, it is highly likely that he was executed on the orders of his own government.*

**Ballistically, as this was a single shot fired at a moving target with an immediate lethal effect, it could only have been fired by an experienced marksman with a long-range weapon. The forensic pathologist stated that the angle at which the bullet entered the victim's head suggested that the shot be fired from a great height, and that the shooter was positioned on a balcony or roof with a direct view of the Daguerre Street. As the ballistic experts found no striations on the lethal bullet, this feature is typical of members of the secret services or special forces soldiers, the only ones authorised to use untraceable ammunition."*

After thanking our colleague for his support, Superintendent Langlois summoned Commander Zandowski and me to tell us emphatically that the conclusions of the investigation into the murder of Benjamin Marshall were a defence secret and must not leave our respective offices under any circumstances. He also told us that the slightest breach of confidentiality would result in our immediate dismissal from the Criminal Investigation Department.

Following this warning, conclusions relating to this case were made public at the end of September. It was obviously out of the question to reveal that Benjamin Marshall had worked as a covert agent in Europe for eleven years on behalf of the United States. It was also out of the question to specify that his status, successively as a student and a journalist in influential circles, had only been a cover enabling him to carry out this activity.

In order to respect defence secrecy, the official conclusions of the investigation were stated as follows, without further clarification: "*Benjamin Marshall was eliminated on French territory because of his extensive investigative journalistic work, which had disturbed certain private economic and financial interests*".

This conclusion implicitly suggested that he had been robbed and murdered because his ongoing investigations were disturbing the economic and financial interests of one of the companies he was investigating before his death. As vagueness is also a technique for manipulating public opinion, no one thought it necessary to specify which of these private interests Benjamin Marshall's investigations might have been most damaging to, once published.

This is how diplomatic relations between France and the United States were saved, just a few months before the French president's visit to Uncle Sam's country.

Chapter 15

Giving rise to a psychotrauma

*Arnaud Wagram's account
of events that occurred
in the personal and professional life
of Lauriane Emans in 2022.*

WHEN Lauriane Emans came to see me in September 2023 to tell me about the events that had occurred in her life since she was recruited by the lab in September 2020, she mentioned the illegal confinement in her office of which she had been the victim on 7th December 2021. The trauma generated by this event, which was exceptional, to say the least, in terms of its severity, had caused her such anxiety that, from that, ever since, she felt she had been released from her duty of loyalty to the man who was still her employer at the time.

She added that the fifty thousand euros she had been promised as compensation were not going to change anything. Subsequently, as no-one had ever raised the subject with her again, she thought that, under the influence of the emotion surrounding her illegal confinement at the end of 2021, the Director must have initially taken the initiative alone in submitting this proposal to her, without subsequently succeeding in having it approved by the Board of Directors.

She also explained to me that, at that time, she had suspected the Medical Department of manipulating the results of the clinical trial on ADHD using video games so that the lab could obtain marketing permission for this treatment more quickly.

From January 2022 onwards, Lauriane Emans went to the lab more out of habit than because she enjoyed her work as a transcriber. She had endeavoured to carry out her work, but without any particular investment, whereas before her illegal confinement, she had shown great dedication to her job. If her energy was no longer directed towards her work, it had to be directed towards something else. Faced with the critical situation in which she found herself, her reaction was consistent with that of a subject with a latent inhibition deficit combined with a high intelligence quotient, these two psychological characteristics leading to increased empathy for those suffering, as well as a strong rejection of injustice.

According to this theory, of which she was unaware but which I could clearly see emerging in her pathological profile, Lauriane Emans had decided, on the one hand, that it was her duty to denounce the manipulation of the results of the clinical trial, in order to avoid a health scandal involving minor patients, as well as exploiting their families, given the exorbitant cost of this treatment. On the other hand, her reaction had gradually taken the form of a more or less latent grudge against the lab in general, and its Human Resources Manager in particular, because of all the vexations and humiliations the latter had subjected her to throughout 2021.

Her friend, Pierre Dobriac, had encouraged her on several occasions to talk to a journalist about the events in which she felt herself to be a victim, or of which she felt other people were at risk of becoming victims, and it was through these links between cause and effect that she came to tell the whole story to Benjamin

Marshall. Given his profession and nationality, she had considered him the most likely media voice to ensure the best possible publicity for the case. When he was murdered five months later, she began to think that her confession might have had something to do with this news item, which she was convinced to be the trigger.

From Wednesday, 4th May 2022, the day after the murder, she went to the lab with the constant thought that she was not only working for dishonest people, but perhaps also for murderers. After reading the article about the start of the investigation in a major national newspaper, on Saturday, 7th May 2022, she began to fear being shot in the head. She hoped that, before his death, Benjamin Marshall would have concealed his source in relation to the information she had confided to him, but she couldn't be absolutely sure.

From Monday, 9th May 2022, she had therefore asked her friend Pierre Dobriac to accompany her, on foot, as she covered, in her wheelchair, the kilometre and a half between her home and her place of work. Being specialised in personal and property security, Lauriane Emans chose to ask him to come with her because she felt reassured by the fact that he was by her side on this exposed route, while praying that it wouldn't be him who was shot in the head. In reality, she knew that this escort was not an absolute guarantee against violence. President Kennedy also had a much larger escort on 22nd November 1963, while visiting Dallas, and this did not prevent him from being assassinated!

Lauriane Emans went on to explain that in August 2022, she and Pierre had gone on holiday together again, but because they were each concerned about what they thought to be their respective involvement in this case, they hadn't enjoyed their time together as much as they had done the previous summer.

At the end of September 2022, when the conclusions of the investigation had been published in the newspapers, they vaguely indicated that Benjamin Marshall had been murdered because of one of his journalistic investigations that could have been prejudicial to private economic and financial interests, without any further details.

Lauriane Emans and Pierre Dobriac were never sure whether it was this journalist's investigation into the lab that had led to his murder, or whether it was the result of another, equally disturbing, investigation that Benjamin Marshall might have been working on at the time. Without first consulting each other, they both drew the conclusion from this information, ambiguous, to say the least, that he had been murdered because of Lauriane's revelations about the lab.

From that time onwards, each of them developed a psychotraumatism linked, on the one hand, to the remorse and guilt of possibly being, to varying degrees, responsible for this tragedy and, on the other hand, to the fact that they never felt safe when they travelled outside their respective homes.

Chapter 16

The truth about the lab case

October 2022,

Third Judicial Police Department,

Yanaël Marceau's recounting

of the hearings of the protagonists

in the lab case.

O N THE BASIS of the documents seized during the police search of the lab, the internal investigation report drawn up by its staff representatives and the testimony of Lauriane Emans, on Monday, 3rd October 2022, Commander Zandowski and I summoned the Director, the Director of Medical Affairs and the Human Resources Manager to hear them as witnesses.

Their respective hearings gave rise to the following minutes:

<u>MINUTES OF THE HEARING IN THE PRESENCE OF HIS LAWYER OF THE LABORATORY'S DIRECTOR OF MEDICAL AFFAIRS BY JPOs COMMANDER ZANDOWSKI AND INSPECTOR MARCEAU, MONDAY, 3RD OCTOBER 2022, THIRD JUDICIAL POLICE DEPARTMENT</u>

JPOs: Sir, we have studied the evaluation forms of the minor patients taking part in the clinical trial on the treatment of ADHD using video games. The results appear to be identical on each of these forms, as if they had been duplicated from one patient to another. How do you explain this?

The Medical Director: We do not duplicate results from one patient to another. The protocol for this clinical trial has been designed in such a way that the first signs of progress appear in minor patients after the first three months of treatment.

JPOs: As this treatment is offered to children and teenagers of different ages, each of whom may have been suffering from different symptoms of ADHD for varying lengths of time, it seems fairly strange to us that the progress recorded in each patient is all at the same stage, without any discrimination as to age, the nature of the symptoms or the known duration of the disorder. How do you explain this?

The Medical Director: As I have just told you, the protocol has been designed in such a way that the first signs of progress occur at the end of the third month of treatment, in line with a process of brain plasticity. Thereafter, this progress may be strengthened to varying degrees from one patient to the next, depending on their age, initial symptoms and the known duration of their respective suffering condition.

JPOs: We also noticed that you admitted children from the age of three into your clinical trial. Isn't that a bit young to be using them as guinea pigs?

The Medical Director: It's very young indeed, but if we want to find out at what age this treatment is likely to have an effect on the brains of hyperactive children, we have to include children of all ages in our clinical trials.

JPOs: Don't the recommendations of the various national and continental health authorities require you to limit this type of trial to children aged eight and over?

The Medical Director: Absolutely, but these are only recommendations, with no legal effect and consequently no penalty for non-compliance. Now isn't the very purpose of a research and development department in innovative health technologies to cross these limits, in order to be able to study the age at which the treatment being developed may prove effective?

JPOs: Doesn't crossing this boundary by conducting a clinical trial on such minor young patients pose you an ethical problem?

The Medical Director: Rather, it would be the opposite situation that would pose us an ethical problem! Imagine that a family with a child aged between three and eight asked a hospital, or a private practitioner, to treat the child for ADHD. What would the professionals approached answer this family? That no treatment is available until the child is eight? If the child in question is three, this means that the family will have to wait five years before his/her ADHD can be treated.

We know from experience that, depending on the degree of suffering, such a situation can lead to a risk of the child dropping out of school and becoming desocialised, as well as a risk of the family becoming exhausted and desocialised. Among the many testimonies we have gathered from parents of children with ADHD, we have often heard the following sentence: "*Our child is so unruly and disruptive that we no longer dare go out with him in public, nor invite our family or friends to our home, nor accept the slightest invitation from them.*" Do you think this is an enviable situation for families, whereas a treatment is likely to remedy the disorder that is making their lives a living hell?

JPOs: Are you under pressure from your management to market this treatment as quickly as possible?

The Medical Director: As Director of Research and Development, I have to deal with this every week at the Steering Committee meeting. At this meeting, I have to give the Director and all the heads of departments a progress report on our research.

JPOs: How do you cope with this pressure?

The Medical Director: I pass it on to my research teams, who are responsible for finding results.

JPOs: As this private company specialises in innovative health technologies, in the event that your teams are not able to find sufficiently innovative results in relation to the brand image conveyed externally by the laboratory, aren't you tempted to manipulate the results of your research, even at the margins, in order to make them correspond to this image?

The Medical Director: In such a case, we modify our research protocol, but we do not manipulate the results.

JPOs: What does the Director think?

The Medical Director: Of course, he is not happy and he isn't afraid to let us know it!

JPOs: So how do you manage the pressure? We have noticed a high turnover rate within your teams. Do you see a link between the latter and the pressure you are under, from your management, to achieve results?

The Medical Director: Indeed, it's not unusual for us to make one research team redundant in order to recruit another, when the first has failed to produce results. But isn't it the way things are done in all private companies, which are always racing to find results, when the latter aren't there?

JPOs: We are going to have the results of your research into the treatment of ADHD using video games assessed by the French National Authority for Health to check their credibility. If they are found to have been tampered with, the lab risks a heavy penalty, as well as a substantial fine for fraud and misleading commercial practice by means of a service concerning human health. Pending the results of this audit, please remain on French territory in case the examining magistrate needs to examine you during the current procedure.

THE END OF THE HEARING

This was the end of the Medical Director's hearing, who confirmed what Lauriane Emans had told us in her testimony the previous May. The Medical Director's answers also corroborated the transcriptions of what the elected staff members of the Works Council had said about the pressure being put on the laboratory's research and development teams.

At the end of this first hearing, we carry on with the Director's.

<u>MINUTES OF THE HEARING IN THE PRESENCE OF HIS LAWYER OF THE DIRECTOR OF THE LABORATORY BY JPOs COMMANDER ZANDOWSKI AND INSPECTOR MARCEAU, MONDAY, 3rd OCTOBER 2022, THIRD JUDICIAL POLICE DEPARTMENT</u>

JPOs: Sir, we are hearing you today in the procedure related to the clinical trial on ADHD conducted by your research and development teams, as well as in the one linked to the way in which Ms Emans has been treated by your Human Resources Manager since she was recruited in September 2020.

With regard to the ADHD clinical trial, we have strong suspicions of fraud, given the results mentioned on the patient evaluation forms.

The Director: I have no idea what you're talking about. On what evidence do you base such accusations?

JPOs: Here, we are the ones asking the questions! We are relying on the fact that the patient progress assessment forms seem too similar to us, as if they had been duplicated from one patient to another.

The Director: I am not aware of any such practice, but if it were true, it would be contrary to medical ethics. In that case, you should ask the question to the Medical Director under whose authority the R&D team's work.

JPOs: We have already done this, and without admitting to such a practice, the latter seems to indicate that you are putting him under enormous pressure in terms of results so that this treatment gets its marketing permission as quickly as possible. Can you confirm such remarks for us?

The Director: I'm not going to deny that I'm putting a lot of pressure on the heads of departments, and especially on the Director of Research and Development. On the one hand, since this department includes half of our manpower, it is the most important of our company, not only because of staff numbers but also by the nature of its activity. Secondly, it's in accordance with my role as Director to put pressure on the teams, so as to avoid everyone resting on their laurels once they have been recruited. I could give you examples of employees who have recently been recruited, but who merely spend their time in contemplative presenteeism.

JPOs: Which means?

The Director: This means that they are present in the company, but spend most of their time doing things other than the tasks mentioned in their job description. They may consult their smartphone several times a day, some of them compulsively, for reasons completely unrelated to their work, which contributes neither to the productivity of the teams nor to the speed with which results are to be obtained.

JPOs: The Medical Director told us that when a team was unable to produce results quickly enough, it was dismissed and replaced by a newly recruited team. Can you confirm this for us?

The Director: Indeed, I can confirm it; the Medical Director is acting in this way in order to comply with my directives.

JPOs: In scientific research activities, especially those relating to human health, doesn't the fact of obtaining results mean that employees have to work over a long period of time?

The Director: This may well be the case in the public research sector. As far as I'm concerned, I run a private company, financed by shareholders who are anxious to recover their initial outlay at the time of the annual dividend distribution. If this were not possible, they would withdraw the company's capital, which would become an empty shell. That's why, if the employees want to continue working for this company, they have to produce results that are likely to generate sufficient profits to satisfy the shareholders. The pressure I put on the department heads is therefore linked to the pressure I myself am under from our backers. Subsequently, I imagine that the heads of department pass on this pressure to the staff they are responsible for managing. If some of them can't stand it, they are free to leave: we are not holding them back!

JPOs: We are now going to examine you about the Lauriane Emans part of the case. During her hearing, she told us she had been recruited by your company on your initiative. Can you confirm us this information?

The Director: Absolutely, Ms Emans was recommended to me by one of my university friends, who has become a psychiatrist in Toulouse. After two and a half years of therapy following *The Soufflot Street case*, the latter had thought that Ms Emans's integration into a work group would be favourable to her resocialisation. To this end, in June 2020, he sent me her CV, with her agreement. Given the quality of her academic background and her previous experience as a freelance transcriber, I supported her recruitment to the lab, which took effect on Tuesday, 1st September 2020.

JPOs: During her hearing, this employee, who is recognised as a disabled worker, told us that she had been subjected to various forms of vexation and humiliation by the Human Resources Manager throughout 2021. Were you aware of this situation?

The Director: Ms Emans asked me to intervene after the Human Resources Manager had refused to grant her three hours' leave on the day she was due to attend her literary prize-giving ceremony. So I was informed almost in real time of this moment of tension between them. To put an end to it, I gave her these three hours off her work schedule without forcing her to make them up. After that, we regularly passed each other at meetings of the Steering Committee meetings and the Works Council, where, apart from the usual courtesies, we had no further discussions until I was informed on my return from Australia in December 2021 that she had been confined illegally in her office.

In order to hear her version about this accident at work, I went to her home, where she had shut herself away while on sick leave. On this occasion, I discovered the interminable list of all the vexations and humiliations to which she had been subjected by the Human Resources Manager throughout 2021. I then asked her why she hadn't told me about it earlier, but she said she hadn't dared because she had been recruited on my initiative.

JPOs: In your opinion, why did the Human Resources Manager behave in this way towards Ms Emans?

The Director: The HRM and I had a brief affair about ten years ago, which I ended when my wife died in one of the attacks that had plunged Paris into mourning in 2015. So I wouldn't be surprised if she were jealous of the fact that I had myself recruited this employee and that I had done some publicity for her literary prize. After the tragedy she experienced in 2017, which my psychiatrist friend told me about, I think that showing empathy towards her is a matter of simple humanity, but go and make the HRM understand that! She's not driven by compassion!

JPOs: Have you taken any measures against the HRM, since the end of 2021, to ensure that the acts of sabotage concerning Ms Emans's work don't happen again in the future?

The Director: Objectively speaking, as Director, I'm not in a position to do much about the multiple acts of sabotage that the HRM is subjecting Ms Emans to, especially the fact that she gives her badly recorded audio files, or that she opens the door or the window of the meeting room when there is noise nearby.

As far as the regular lift breakdowns are concerned, it's impossible to know whether these are random or intentional. In any case, I don't think the HRM so Machiavellian as to cause lift breakdowns. In order to limit the consequences for Ms Emans, from the beginning of this year I asked the HRM to warn her by SMS on days when, on her arrival at 8 a.m., she noticed that the lift had broken down. As Ms Emans doesn't have to start work before 9 a.m., this precaution means she doesn't have to come in to work for nothing and allows both parties involved starting teleworking for the day in question.

Since the beginning of this year, as the HRM's direct line manager, I have also adopted other protective measures with regard to Ms Emans. Firstly, I demanded the HRM, for fear of disciplinary action, stop changing the dates of meetings at the last minute, as this practice had had the effect of disrupting the schedules of the heads of departments, as well as those of the staff representatives and mine, throughout last year.

Secondly, I also told her that, because of the vendetta she had conducted against Ms Emans in 2021, from 2022 onwards, the latter would be having her annual assessment discussion with me, rather than with her, until further notice.

When Ms Emans confided in me at the end of last year, she also drew my attention to the fact that the HRM was regularly asking her questions that she felt were too personal, encroaching on her private life. Because of her extrovert disposition and the unavoidable position she believes she holds within our lab, the HRM behaves in this way with everyone without realising that her attitude may be an embarrassment for more reserved employees who are anxious not to mix their professional and personal lives. As I was unable to change the HRM's temperament, I advised Ms Emans to practise the art of sidestepping with regard to these indiscreet questions, in the hope that after a while her superior, tired of not getting any answers, would stop bothering her.

With regard to the illegal confinement of Ms Emans in her office, during the internal investigation carried out by the Works Council, the HRM told us that she had activated the building's locking system when we left for Australia at 6:30 p.m. According to her, since non-managerial staff usually leave the building at 6 p.m. and managers all had to leave for Australia with us, she was convinced that when we left the building there was no-one left inside.

Personally, I thought that such carelessness constituted a serious professional misconduct. I then took disciplinary action against her with consequences for her employment contract. In concrete terms, this meant that she was laid off for three days, with loss of pay. I couldn't go any further than that, in terms of punishment: this position constituting an important cog in the wheel of our company, which has six hundred employees, each absence of the HRM is detrimental to the functioning of our team. Moreover, like all people who believe themselves to be essential, she never shies away from pointing this out to us! To tell you the truth, when she was absent, I was the one who had to take on her job, as well as my own, as the managerial duties were not doubled, as you can imagine!

JPOs: You have just mentioned the fact that the illegal confinement of Ms Emans in her office was due to the negligence of the HRM. This suggests that by activating the door locking system, she wouldn't have intended to illegally confine Ms Emans to her office for several hours. However, given the litigation that had developed between the two of them over the previous twelve months, wouldn't it be more appropriate to talk about a deliberate offence?

The Director: I confess that the thought has crossed my mind, but as I have no means of proving such an intention, I prefer to leave it to the judicial investigation to establish it, should it be proven.

JPOs: If this were the case, would you consider dismissing your HRM and recruiting another one?

The Director: Objectively, I should proceed in this way, but as the French Labour Code doesn't allow me to punish the same employee twice for the same offence, I couldn't impose a suspension lay-off pending the dismissal of the HRM, knowing that I had already imposed a disciplinary suspension lay-off on her. I would be even less likely to do so, given that recruiting such an important executive for a company like ours can take weeks or even months of searching. Finally, once the executive has taken up his position, as HRM, he is usually responsible for recruiting employees, both managerial and non-managerial.

JPOs: Be that as it may, as the company's legal representative, you risk a very heavy sentence before the criminal court, on the one hand, for inexcusable fault on the part of the employer, in the sense that you should have been aware of the danger that this situation caused to Ms Emans's health and safety and that you took no steps to prevent this accident at work. On the other hand, you also run the risk of being heavily sentenced for the anxiety that the latter caused to Ms Emans, an employee protected by the Labour Code because of her disability, and for the recruitment of which you had previously been given financial incentives and social benefits.

The Director: Indeed, but as I had delegated to the HRM the authority to manage employees, including their health and safety at work, as the person in charge, she will have to answer to the courts about this situation.

THE END OF THE HEARING

In this way, the Director of the lab, passing on the responsibility for the offences we were accusing him of, to the Medical Director and to the Human Resources Manager, skilfully exonerated himself in the two cases we heard about from him, that day! He had every right to do so, under the delegations of power he had previously granted them, provided that he had given them the means to practise them and also provided that these two executives had the authority and the competence necessary to practise their respective delegations of power. This was certainly the angle from which their respective lawyers would try to defend each of them.

After hearing the Director, we carried on by hearing the lab's Human Resources Manager.

<u>MINUTES OF THE HEARING IN THE PRESENCE OF HIS LAWYER OF THE LABORATORY'S HUMAN RESOURCES MANAGER BY JPOs COMMANDER ZANDOWSKI AND INSPECTOR MARCEAU, MONDAY, 3rd OCTOBER 2022, THIRD JUDICIAL POLICE DEPARTMENT</u>

JPOs: Madam, we are hearing from you today, in the case of the laboratory, about the illegal confinement of Ms Emans in her office, which occurred on Tuesday, 7th December 2021.

As these events constitute both an accident at work and various breaches of the Penal Code, the Labour Inspector has forwarded the internal investigation report drawn up by the staff representatives to the Public Prosecutor. What can you tell us about the origins of this incident, for which this document suggests that you were responsible?

The HRM: That day, as all the managers had left the building at 6:30 p.m. to go to the airport to board a flight to Australia, and all the non-managerial employees usually left the building at 6 p.m., I thought there was nobody left inside and activated the door locking system.

JPOs: However, Ms Emans was still at her desk and, according to her statement, she was supposed to work there until 7:53 p.m. that day, as she did every Tuesday and Thursday evening. Didn't you know that?

The HRM: As the company's annual congress, organised by the parent company, had been cancelled the year before because of Covid-19, all the managers were absolutely determined to attend last year's conference, and I was no exception. As a result, in the rush and excitement of leaving for Australia, it no longer occurred to me that Ms Emans had to stay later than usual that evening.

JPOs: According to her statement, it was you who, when she was recruited, asked her to work until 7:53 p.m., on these two days, as a replacement for the hours she couldn't work when she left the office at 4:45 p.m., on Mondays, Wednesdays and Fridays, in order to go to her physiotherapy sessions. Do you confirm her testimony on this point?

The HRM: Absolutely, I can confirm that.

JPOs: This situation, repeated every week, was therefore not unusual for you, and it was all the less so because it was you who decided to organise Ms Emans's schedule in this way. So how could you fail to notice that she was still inside the building that evening?

The HRM: As I've just told you, with the departure for Australia, we weren't in the usual routine, which made me forget about this particular employee.

JPOs: However, as Ms Emans was not one of the company's executives, she didn't go to the airport with you to board the flight to Australia, did she?

The HRM: Absolutely, I can confirm that.

JPOs: If she wasn't in the group of executives leaving for the airport, she had to have been somewhere that day when you left the building, didn't she?

The HRM: Exactly, but I didn't think about the fact that it was Tuesday and that she had to stay late at the office.

JPOs: In your position as a manager, you are still supposed to think about the consequences of your actions on the staff management. In this case, at the time of the events, Ms Emans had been working with you for fifteen months. You might therefore have been used to seeing her leave the office at 7:53 p.m., every Tuesday and Thursday evening, which makes your error of assessment all the less excusable.

The HRM: Even though she works in my department, I don't keep an eye on her comings and goings, and she doesn't come and say "goodnight" to me when she leaves her office at 7:53 p.m., on Tuesday and Thursday evenings!

JPOs: Is activating the electronic door locking system usually part of your duties?

The HRM: Usually, like all managers, I finish my day at 8 p.m., after eleven hours' work. At that time, as no one is supposed to be on the premises, the security company responsible for guarding them activates the system, after checking that no employees are still inside.

JPOs: If this duty is usually carried out by the security company in charge of their surveillance, why did you assume the latter on that day?

The HRM: I thought that, with no-one left inside the building, we couldn't just leave it wide open for an hour and a half, until the security company closed the doors at 8 p.m.!

JPOs: Of course, but before doing so, didn't you check that anyone was still inside?

The HRM: I didn't have at my disposal the video surveillance resources that the security company usually uses to carry out these checks.

JPOs: In that case, it wasn't up to you to make such a decision, was it?

The HRM: That's easy to say in with hindsight.

JPOs: The Director told us that he had given you the authority to manage the health and safety of employees when they are in the workplace during working hours. However, this authority doesn't include the fact that you be responsible for the safety of the building. If you had been absolutely determined to close the building, you would have had to ask the security company to ensure that no employees were left inside, wouldn't you?

The HRM: Of course I should have, but I didn't!

JPOs: Why didn't you take this elementary safety measure? Do you have any particular grievance towards Ms Emans?

The HRM: I don't have any special grievance towards her.

JPOs: But that's not what she told us during her hearing: according to her, when she was hired, you did nothing to help her to integrate. Can you confirm this?

The HRM: It's true that when she first joined the company, I didn't get involved in organising her integration. In fact, I didn't really appreciate the fact that this employee had been imposed on me by the Director. Usually, I am responsible for recruiting staff for the various departments, by submitting the files of the successful candidates to the Director beforehand so that he can approve their recruitment. In this case, not only did the Director initiate her recruitment, but he never asked my opinion on the matter whereas she was due to join my own department!

JPOs: From the beginning of 2021, you allegedly subjected this employee, who is recognised as a disabled worker, to various forms of harassment, such as refusing to grant her two and a half hours' absence from work to enable her to attend her literary prize-giving ceremony on Thursday, 28th January 2021. Can you confirm these facts?

The HRM: Absolutely, I can confirm that. Ms Emans was already taking liberties with the group timetable to get to her physiotherapy sessions three times a week at the end of the day. So I couldn't see why I should have granted her another one.

JPOs: Nevertheless she had offered to come to work on a Saturday morning, in order to make up the hours she couldn't have done on the working days that week, hadn't she?

The HRM: Yes, but I thought she was being a bit too liberal with the planning. So I refused to do her this favour.

JPOs: As the person in charge of the employees' community, didn't you assess the positive dynamic that receiving this prize could generate in terms of integration among her colleagues?

The HRM: No, I didn't see it that way, because I thought that this distinction was part of her private activity and not part of the work she was doing for the lab.

JPOs: Your director didn't react in the same way and gave this prize a lot of publicity, according to what she told us, didn't he?

The HRM: Exactly. If you ask me, I thought he was a bit overenthusiastic about it, but in any case, from that day on, everyone understood that the Director really liked her.

JPOs: As he told us that you had once had a relationship with him, would you have felt any bitterness towards Ms Emans as a result?

The HRM: Yes, but not to the extent of voluntarily and illegally confining her in her office, if that's what you're asking.

JPOs: In view of the prior litigation between you and Ms Emans at the time of the events, it is not impossible that the examining magistrate will requalify this illegal confinement as an intentional offence. Be that as it may, given the delegation of power you received from your Director, you will have to answer personally, before the criminal court, for the employer's unforgivable fault about what the court considers to be an accident at work and, moreover, involving a disabled employee.

The HRM: I certainly hope that the Director gets it in the neck too! After all, it was he who initiated her recruitment and there's no way I'm going to take the full responsibility for this situation!

THE END OF THE HEARING

That was the end of the hearing of the Human Resources Manager, who was clearly not ready to accept the fact that she had herself originated the offences she was accused of. The judge and ourselves knew that only an exemplary sanction would be likely to prevent any repetition of such behaviours on her part in the future.

At this stage of the investigation, we did not yet know that a sanction of a different nature, and with a far more devastating effect than judicial sentences, was going to fall on the laboratory at the end of 2022.

Chapter 17

Big Pharma, Big Drama, Managing is not a game

December 2022,

Yanaël Marceau's recounting

of various events that occurred

during the second half of 2022.

T HE MONTH OF DECEMBER 2022 should have ended the year of treatment that my son, Little Adrien, has been receiving at Necker Hospital for his ADHD. However, during the previous summer holidays, when he had just turned four and was expressing himself better and better, he had explained to Camille, his mum: "*At nursery school, one of my classmates has been teasing me all the time.*" Together, we asked him why this child had teased him, and he replied that it was because he had told her, on the first day of school, that his father was a policeman.

We then realised that his disruptive and agitated behaviour during school hours had been a reaction to this harassment, and at the end of July we decided to put an end to his treatment with video games. After seven months of therapy, this had produced no effect on our son, apart from the tiredness he felt having to travel across Paris with his babysitter to get to the Necker Hospital three times a week. Since he had told us about the situation he had been in, we had also realised that this treatment would be no more beneficial to him in the future than it had been up to that point.

In August, when the three of us were on a summer holiday, talking about the start of the new school year, Little Adrien, traumatised by this harassment, told us that he didn't want to go back to school any more. To prevent him from developing a school phobia, we quickly had him transferred to another school, and since September 2022, things had been back to normal: every late afternoon, our son would come home from school, fulfilled, after his day in the middle section, and we had heard nothing more about ADHD or any similar disorder.

At the same time as these personal events, there were other significant developments in my professional life. Firstly, in September, the investigation into the assassination of Benjamin Marshall had been concluded, with the support of a commander of the Criminal Squad, in a way that was unexpected, to say the least, and which would never be revealed to the general public. These conclusions, which were classified as a defence secret and were accepted by the highest political authorities on both sides of the Atlantic, helped to preserve the bilateral relationship between France and the United States.

On the other hand, in October, Commander Zandowski and I heard the Director, as well as two of the managers on whom he had clearly decided to shift all responsibility for the incidents revealed by our investigation. At the end of November, the case was still being investigated, pending the results of the audit conducted by the French National Authority for Health into the evaluation sheets for the clinical trial on the treatment of ADHD using video games.

The end of November also coincided with the State visit by the President of the French Republic and his wife to the United States, from 30th November to 2nd December 2022. Before their departure, the Regional Director of the Judicial Police had given the Minister of the Interior the article written by Benjamin Marshall on the various failures and breaches of the laboratory, which Lauriane Emans had revealed to him eleven months earlier. The Minister of the Interior then passed it on to the President of the Republic who, on his arrival on American soil, entrusted it, like a relic, to the President of the United States.

Shortly after this State visit, on Thursday, 8th December 2022, the day when the French weeklies came out, all the printed and online media edited that day, in France and the United States, published in tribute to Benjamin Marshall the article he had written on the subject before his assassination.

The latter, lined with a black mourning crêpe, appeared on the front page of each of these newspapers and websites, and was presented as follows:

BIG PHARMA, BIG DRAMA – MANAGING IS NOT A GAME

"According to an anonymous source, a clinical trial is currently underway in a private US laboratory with the aim of developing a treatment using video games to treat attention deficit disorder with or without hyperactivity, more commonly known as ADHD, in minor patients of industrialised countries.

This laboratory, which specialises in research and development in the field of innovative health technologies, was founded in New York in 2000, and has set up subsidiaries in Canada, Japan, Australia, Germany and France. To date, the combined workforce of these different structures amounts to five thousand people, a quarter of whom are responsible for the company's support functions (human resources management, communications, accounting and financial management, logistics, IT) and the remaining three quarters of whom are made up of teams of researchers equally divided between the discovery of an innovative treatment for Covid-19 and that of a treatment likely to cure ADHD.

ADHD is characterised by behaviours of inattention, impulsivity and/or hyperactivity, most often generated by a neurodevelopmental problem that affects the patient from birth. In this hypothesis, the longer the patient is affected, the more difficult it becomes to treat him, as the ADHD has had time to become deeply ingrained in his neuropsychological functioning.

Such a disorder may also arise in reaction to a particularly stressful psychosocial incident (parental divorce, family bereavement, harassment, social or intra-family violence, etc.), in a young patient who has no other psychological resources to cope with it. If this is the case, only a change of situation can put an end to the patient's symptoms, so the therapy through video games may prove ineffective, useless or even harmful. However, according to some families, the evaluation questionnaire they were given before their child or adolescent was included in this clinical trial did not give them any opportunity to mention elements relating to a particular psychosocial context likely to explain the onset of this behavioural disorder in the patient being tested.

Whatever the origin of ADHD, its prevalence has exploded since the early 2000s, affecting up to 5% of children and adolescents in industrialised countries, without it being possible to determine precisely the factors behind this explosion. The only certainty is that it constitutes the disease of the 21st century, in the same way that backache and depression symbolically represent the diseases of the 20th. Such a high prevalence rate gives us a glimpse of the colossal financial stakes involved in developing this treatment.

This is the context in which, since January 2022, it has been the subject of a clinical trial in France, Germany, Australia, Japan, Canada and the United States. The trial is due to last one year and will involve one thousand minor patients in each of these *countries, bringing the total cohort to six thousand. The minors selected are aged between three and eighteen, in order to widen the laboratory's target group of potential customers as much as possible, should the trial result in a treatment.*

In order to benefit from this treatment, patients have to go to an approved hospital three times a week for a half-hour therapy session. As this treatment has not yet been validated by the national or continental health authorities, it is not reimbursed by the health insurance systems. As the establishments testing it are charged ten thousand euros per patient, it is their families who ultimately have to bear this exorbitant cost.

This experiment has another major flaw: according to an internal source from staff representatives, the laboratory's management has instructed the Director of Medical Affairs to have the researchers in charge of this clinical trial fill in all the patient evaluation forms in the same way. In concrete terms, this procedure mentions the occurrence of initial progress after three months of treatment, without distinction as to age, the known duration of the disorder, or the nature of the symptoms presented by the patient being evaluated. However, ADHD is protean, patients may be affected by one or even two of the three characteristic symptoms, combined to varying degrees, depending on the nature of the impairment from which they suffer. Similarly, some patients may be affected by all three symptoms combined (inattention, hyperactivity, impulsivity) to varying degrees, so that ADHD may take twenty-seven different forms. Nevertheless, the research results do not show such extensive distinctions in relation to these various combinations.

These are the breaches of medical ethics for which the company must now take responsibility, but they are not the only ones: according to information relayed a year before by our colleagues in the French press, the laboratory could also be the source of failures in staff management and compliance with employment law, as demonstrated by the illegal confinement in its office of one of its employees who had been previously recognised as a disabled worker.

The events are said to have taken place on Tuesday, 7th December 2021. On that day, all the managers of the French subsidiary travelled together to Roissy-Charles-de-Gaulle airport to board a flight to Australia, where, at the end of the week, the brand's annual conference, organised by the parent company and bringing together the managers of all its subsidiaries, was due to take place. During this collective departure, at 6:30 p.m., the Human Resources Manager allegedly activated the electronic system for closing the building's doors, while a disabled employee remained inside the building. According to a schedule drawn up for the latter by the same Human Resources Manager, she was to work until 7:53 p.m. that day, as she did every Tuesday and Thursday evening.

The latter, who was responsible for transcribing the minutes of the meetings of the Works Council and the Steering Committee, had been reporting to this Human Resources Manager for fifteen months at the time of the events. It is therefore difficult to understand how such a misunderstanding could have occurred, unless it was intentional, especially because, according to an internal source from the employee representatives, the HRM had been involved in a personal litigation with this disabled person since she had been recruited in September 2020. This tense situation is said to have led the HRM to bully, abuse and humiliate this employee throughout 2021. Her illegal confinement would merely constitute the culmination of a conflict situation that was already well underway in this department, but to which no one would have paid any attention until the fateful date of 7th December 2021.

On the day in question, the security company responsible for monitoring the building was unable to remotely deactivate the locking system of the building's doors, so the employee and her electric wheelchair had to return to the ground from the tenth floor, where her office was located, in the first rescuers' basket. Beforehand, the latter had to cut out the window using extrication equipment, which set off the alarm and caused panic in the whole district for an hour.

When questioned about these various breaches and failures, the laboratory's management did not bother giving us its version of the facts. However, although its managers do not wish to speak to the press, they will have to answer for their actions when these two cases come to trial before the Paris Criminal Court in 2023.

We will keep you informed on further developments in our future editions."

Benjamin Marshall

(9th November 1989 - 3rd May 2022)

Article published posthumously

Lies, bankruptcy and idleness

December 2023
Arnaud Wagram's recounting of events
following the publication
of Benjamin Marshall's article
in France and the United States.

I AM NOW going to tell you how the story Lauriane Emans told me ended when she came to see me in September 2023, and what the consequences were for the various protagonists.

In December 2022, the posthumous publication of Benjamin Marshall's article on both sides of the Atlantic damaged the laboratory's reputation. During the Christmas holidays of 2022-2023, at festive meals all over the world, the information revealed by this article, which left no one indifferent, was widely commented on by the families of patients, but also by those who were in no way concerned by the health scandal relating to the treatment of ADHD by video games.

From a legal point of view, at the end of the investigation into this part of the case, in January 2023, the laboratory would have had to appear before the Criminal Court of Paris for fraud and the offence of misleading commercial practice by means of a service linked to human health. In order to avoid tarnishing its brand image through the bad publicity that a trial would have caused, its Director, its Financial Director and its lawyers undertook to negotiate an out-of-court settlement with the French justice. This amounted to ten million euros and had to be paid out from the company's own funds to the French Public Revenue Office. The families of the patients had also decided to form a class action with the aim of obtaining compensation for their loss and harm. Thus, at that time, the laboratory had not yet finished with the French courts or with the financial compensation. On an individual level, the Director of Medical Affairs was banned for life from managing research teams.

With regard to the illegal confinement of Lauriane Emans, even though she had not wished to take part in the legal procedure, the Public Prosecutor's Office took over the case on its own initiative, in accordance with the principle of discretionary prosecution set out in article 40 of the Code of Criminal Procedure. The laboratory should therefore have been sentenced by the criminal court for the employer's inexcusable fault, for anxiety caused to a vulnerable employee, and also for disturbing public order by setting off the building's alarm, which had caused an uproar throughout the neighbourhood for an hour. To avoid further damage to the company's brand image, the Director, the Financial Director and the company's lawyers decided once again to negotiate an out-of-court settlement with the French courts. This amounted to five million euros and had to be paid out from the laboratory's funds to the French Public Revenue Office. On an individual level, the Human Resources Manager Director was banned for life from managing employees.

Faced with this crisis, in March 2023, the top managers of the laboratory had agreed that it would be better to close the European subsidiaries, whose medical legislation and employment law they found too restricting. They then had asked those of their European managers who agreed to do so to move to the United States. At the same time, they also closed the subsidiaries in Japan, Australia and Canada, leaving only the head office in New York.

The aim of this strategy of returning to the United States had been to position the laboratory in the North American market for the discovery of an innovative vaccine against Covid-19. However, as the United States is traditionally very pernickety when it comes to corporate social responsibility, particularly with regard to disabled workers, the Human Resources Manager's actions towards Lauriane Emans and the medical director's breaches of ethics were not in the company's favour in the eyes of the American health authorities.

It had been therefore decided, at the highest level, that, from spring 2023, the company would be expelled from all invitations to tender in the US healthcare sector. As it would no longer be authorised to market new patents for innovative healthcare technologies, the company would have to live on its past achievements. Nevertheless, its old patents having fallen into the public domain twenty years after they had been registered, treatments based on the innovative technologies that the laboratory had discovered in the early 2000s could now be copied by its competitors and marketed by them at lower cost. This strategy of returning to its country of origin had therefore also proved to be in vain.

Defeated by this accumulation of more than unfavourable circumstances, the company was gradually heading towards bankruptcy and, in June 2023, had to lay off its entire staff, which still amounted to one thousand of the five thousand it had employed when it was still managing its foreign subsidiaries.

Among these thousand people was Mrs Z, Pierre Dobriac's former companion, who had opportunely left France for the United States on 7th September 2017, the same day that Pierre Dobriac disappeared in *The Soufflot Street case*. At the beginning of July 2023, she returned to France, and as soon as she set foot in the country, she went straight to Pierre Dobriac's home. Knowing that before she left for the United States, she had been employed by the laboratory, which had recently gone bankrupt, he was not surprised to see her and without further ado, they decided to resume their life together, as if nothing had happened six years earlier.

Pierre Dobriac, still psychologically disturbed by what he believed to be his involvement in the murder of Benjamin Marshall, because of the advice he had given Lauriane Emans to tell her story to a journalist, didn't find the courage to rebel against his former companion's new intrusion into his life. From then on, everything between them went back to the way it had been before, with Mrs Z constantly extending her control over his professional and personal life.

As soon as she was informed of his return, by a text message sent to her by Pierre Dobriac announcing the cancellation of a holiday they had planned to spend together in the next August, Lauriane Emans understood that, as a result of this control over him, their nights out to the cinema, the theatre, concerts and restaurants, as well as their moments of sharing and discussing the important issues of life, were now over.

Deeply convinced that she was the cause of Benjamin Marshall's murder, because of the story of the lab she had told him in detail, she didn't find the strength to fight to try and keep alive the friendship that bound her to the man who had come with her from her home to work, each morning and conversely each afternoon, from May 2022 to March 2023, that is to say for almost a year, until the shutting down of the French subsidiary. As a result, instead of enjoying the Atlantic coast with her friend, as had been the case during the previous two months of August, Lauriane spent her summer holidays alone and shut away in her flat.

In September, she decided to spend a few days with her family, who lived in the Occitanie region of France and, on this occasion, she made an appointment at my surgery. I thought it was just a courtesy visit, due to her passing through Toulouse, but over the course of several consultations, she began to tell me this long story. As she went on, in disbelief, I asked her if she hadn't started writing a new detective story, the script of which she would have been recounting me, prolonging the suspense slightly more at each session. She swore to me that this was not the case, and advised me to read various articles in the national press about the lab affair and the murder of Benjamin Marshall.

After finding out on the Internet that what she had told me was true, I suddenly realised that, during her first therapy session, it was I who had suggested that she write *A Case For The Paris Police*, the novel for which she had won the literary prize through which she had met Benjamin Marshall.

I also realised that I had helped to recruit her to the laboratory, through the resocialisation advice I had given her in 2020, at the end of her therapy. I could not for a moment have suspected the linking of unfortunate events that this recruitment would lead to: the ill-treatment of Lauriane by the Human Resources Manager, her direct superior, the murder of Benjamin Marshall, the only American journalist ever to be killed on French territory since the Second World War, the bankruptcy of the laboratory and the redundancy of five thousand employees, the return of Mrs Z to France and, as a result, the loss of the man Lauriane had considered her best friend since she had seen him again in February 2021.

Unable to overcome the weight of remorse and guilt that came over me from the moment I became aware of all this history for which I felt partly responsible, three months later, in December 2023, I decided to unscrew my psychiatrist's plaque, after only twenty years of practice.

In the months that followed, having retired from my private practice, I no longer heard from Lauriane Emans, but knowing her initial psychological fragility, I wondered whether she would ever be able to recover from such an ordeal. At the same time, I knew that because of her emotional hypersensitivity, she couldn't stand injustice, lies or duplicity, which had led her to denounce the scandal of the ADHD treatment and, at the same time, all the abuse she had suffered in the lab, in order to prevent it from happening to other people in the future.

In the end, she never received the fifty thousand euros in compensation promised to her by the Director two years earlier.

Worse still, she had lost her best friend, as well as her first job which should have allowed her to take advantage of a less precarious and more materially comfortable existence.

However, her fortitude had led her to put aside her personal comfort to denounce failures that could have led to a health scandal involving minor patients.

She had sacrificed herself for a cause more important than herself.

Was it worth the risk?

Only time will tell.

The genesis
of this detective novel

THIS STORY was inspired by some of the incredible situations I found myself in while studying or trying to enter the world of work as a person with reduced mobility using an electric wheelchair outside the home. It is also the fruit of my imagination, which developed from various books and articles that I read while preparing to write this book, a list of which is given below:

***Works :**

- DELCOURT, Thierry, *La fabrique des enfants anormaux*, Max Milo Éditions, Collection Essais-Documents, 2021, 213 p.

- HUNTER, Mark, *Le journalisme d'investigation aux États-Unis et en France*, PUF, Collection Que sais-je?, 1997, 118 p. (Available only in Kindle format, the printed version has not been republished).

- KERDELLANT, Christine, *Histoire des grandes erreurs de management*, Éditions Denoël, Collection Folio Actuel, 2016, 280 p.

- MARTINET, Pierre, *DGSE : Service Action, Un agent secret sort de l'ombre*, Éditions J'ai Lu, Collection Témoignage, 2012, 380 p.

- Collective work by several French investigative journalists, *Informer n'est pas un délit : Ensemble contre les nouvelles censures*, Éditions Calmann-Lévy, Collection Documents, Actualités, Société, 2015, 155 p.

*Articles:

-GAON, Thomas and STORA, Michel, *Soigner des jeux vidéo/Soigner par les jeux vidéo, Regards croisés sur un révélateur de mal-être*, OpenEdition Journals, *Quaderni*, No. 67, Autumn 2008, pp. 33-42.

https://doi.org/10.4000/quadermi.192/

- GABRIEL, Guillaume, *The use of video games in the treatment of young people with disabilities*, 21st April 2021.

https://cursus.edu/fr/22639/lutilisation-des-jeux-video-dans-le-traitement-de-jeunes-en-situation-de-handicap

- HODENT-VILLAMAN, Célia, *Are video games good for the brain? Sciences humaines* No. 178, January 2007.

https://www.scienceshumaines.com/les-jeux-video-sont-ils-bons-pour-le-cerveau_fr_15191.html

- L'influx.com Site, *Le jeu vidéo: cause de troubles ou outil thérapeutique,* November 2018.

https://www.linflux.com/sciences/le-jeu-video-cause-de-troubles-ou-outil-therapeutique/

- Néozone Site, *Les médecins peuvent prescrire ce jeu vidéo pour soigner les troubles de l'attention,* 10th April 2002.

https://www.neozone.org/mobilite/les-medecins-peuvent-prescrire-ce-jeu-video-pour-soigner-les-troubles-de-lattention/

> A few words
from the author

M Y NAME IS Laurence Sellin. I was born in 1972. I live in the Gers (France) and work as a freelance transcriber for legal meetings.

I would like to thank everyone who gave me their support, advice and encouragement during the writing of this detective novel, especially my beta readers.

I would also like to thank my closest relatives, who gave me a taste for reading when I was very young, and my readers, without whom this book would not be possible. I hope you enjoy reading it as much as I enjoyed writing it.

If you would like to personally tell me what you think of the book, you can send me your comments directly by going to the following page of my website, where a contact form is available for this purpose:

https://www.editionspolarimpulse.com/class.html

If you wish to write a public commentary or review about the book, I would be very grateful to receive it from you by e-mail, at contact@editionspolarimpulse.com, so that I can read it before it is published on platforms.

You can access the book's review page on Amazon at the following link:

https://www.amazon.fr/review/create-review?asin=2487394005

You can also access it by flashing the following QR Code:

You can access the book's review page on Goodreads at the following link:

https://www.goodreads.com/review/new/204505154-big-pharma-big-drama---managing-is-not-a-game

You can also access it by flashing the following QR Code:

If you would like to join my community of regular readers, you can use the contact form mentioned above to subscribe to the newsletter I send out to people interested in my books, usually at the beginning of the month. In it, I talk about my writing activities, as well as the development of the *Polar Impulse* publishing house, which I set up in January 2023. By subscribing to this newsletter, you will be able to read the latest news about my books every month. Moreover, to thank you for your interest in my publishing work, I will e-mail you a list of my one hundred and fifty favourite novels, most of them psychological thrillers.

Finally, if you are interested in reading the continuation of Yanaël Marceau's investigations and Lauriane Emans's misadventures, the third part of this trilogy is due to be published at the end of 2024.

You can access my author page via the following link:

https://www.amazon.fr/~/e/B0BR61WPB5

Laurence Sellin – Lectoure (Gers) – December 2023.

www.ingramcontent.com/pod-product-compliance
Lightning Source LLC
LaVergne TN
LVHW020334200726
843507LV00012B/2352